· Solus ·

· Solus ·

A Montana Mystery Featuring Gabriel Du Pré

PETER BOWEN

OPEN ROAD

INTEGRATED MEDIA

NEW YORK

Copyright © 2018 by Peter Bowen

Cover design by Ian Koviak

978-1-5040-5091-3

Published in 2018 by Open Road Integrated Media, Inc.
180 Maiden Lane
New York, NY 10038
www.openroadmedia.com

For Steve and Libby Bodio, the Eagle Dreamers

· Solus ·

· Chapter 1 ·

DU PRÉ LOOKED AT the young doctor who was looking at a file on his computer screen. It was Du Pré's file.

. . . I like paper. Ink . . . thought Du Pré. Computers. Shit.

"It looks very good, Mister Du Pré," said the young doctor.

. . . Looks like he is about fifteen . . . thought Du Pré.

"It was malignant but it is a slow-growing carcinoma, fairly common and easily removed. There were no cells in the margins that were occult," said the young doctor.

. . . That does it . . . thought Du Pré . . . They sacrifice chickens here, read the guts. Occult . . .

Du Pré stood up. "Thank you," he said.

"You're very welcome," said the young doctor. The name on his plastic tag was GHOSH.

Du Pré left the office, walked down the hall, his boots screeking on the polished green linoleum tiles.

Madelaine was sitting in Du Pré's old Crown Victoria, beading a small medicine pouch.

"I don't go in those places, Du Pré," she had said. "I find myself in one of those places, I was carried there, unconscious."

Du Pré got in.

"You are dying?" said Madelaine. The tip of her tongue was stuck in the left corner of her mouth.

She was looking at the bead she was setting.

"I got a week maybe," said Du Pré. "They did everything that they could."

"Start the fucking car," said Madelaine. "Anybody stays in Billings ten minutes longer than they have to will not last very long."

As soon as they left the fug of refinery stink Billings sank behind the hills. Du Pré reached under the seat, took out a bottle of whiskey, had a good pull, rolled a smoke, lit it, handed it to Madelaine for the one puff she took from time to time.

"I am glad you are all right," said Madelaine. "You would be very hard to replace. Not impossible, no, but probably pretty hard, so I am very glad you have not got some terrible disease."

"Thank you," said Du Pré. "It is the people who love you who pull you through these terrible times. Their prayers and shit."

"Fuck!" said Madelaine, looking at a bright bead of blood on her fingertip. "I know better than this beading while you are driving."

"*Non*," said Du Pré, "you don't. Obviously, you don't know better. Do not get blood, my car seats . . ."

Du Pré's cruiser was over twenty years old, had four doors from four different cars, all blue and none matching, and the seat upholstery looked like it had been attacked by starving badgers certain there was a nice fat gopher in it somewhere.

"Yah," said Madelaine, mopping the blood from her fingertip off on a scrap of upholstery. "Now I will get gangrene. Bart has all those nice new cars, more'n he needs, he would give you one."

"I don't want, new car," said Du Pré.

"What's that *smell*," said Madelaine, "rubber or burning goatshit, something, are we on fire?"

"It was just a carcinoma," said Du Pré, "not much."

Madelaine laughed.

"You always get that look, you find a doctor who is too young," she said. "You want them old, like Benetsee, have a white lab coat, be about one hundred twenty, you are getting old, Du Pré."

"He looks about fifteen," said Du Pré.

"Oh, Du Pré is so much better," said Madelaine. "Last time he is saying, bitching, that doctor is *twelve*, I should demand ID, that is Du Pré."

"This one was maybe fifteen," said Du Pré.

"And you go to court, pay the speeding ticket a month ago?" said Madelaine.

Du Pré laughed.

"You come back, say you go early, see what the offer is, there is this pretty blond child should be out selling Girl Scout cookies but she is an assistant district attorney . . ." said Madelaine. "Old goat, you should go up in the mountains, live in a cave."

"*Non*," said Du Pré, "they are damp." He had another pull at the whiskey. An ambulance went past in the other lanes, heading toward Billings. A few miles farther on, there was a clutch of emergency vehicles and a fire truck, and two Highway Patrol cars, lights flashing.

A big sedan was upside down on top of a fence; a pickup truck was a blackened hulk, smoking a little.

Madelaine crossed herself and her lips moved. Du Pré rolled another smoke. They got to the road north and they turned off. Now it was two lanes all the way home.

The sun was still high, there would be daylight.

A low mountain range came into view to the west, a smoky lavender and dark gray on the horizon. Du Pré got up to speed.

One-ten, a Montanan's answer to a hell of a lot of not much. Du Pré slowed when he came to the tops of hills. You never knew when a rancher with a tractor and a big load of hay would be moving at twenty miles an hour just out of sight.

Or some dumb cow would have gotten through a fence and be standing ready to crush the radiator and, at the speeds Du Pré drove, intimately commingle all its flesh with the car.

Du Pré looked out the window, saw a big yellow-gray coyote trot to a hilltop, pause, look back. The coyote would drop out of sight if the car slowed down.

Du Pré slowed more as the crest came up to flat and the coyote vanished.

"Pallas is bad," said Madelaine. "Where is that old bastard Benetsee? We need him now. He pisses me off, he always shows up when we need him but he has not done that. He is dead maybe."

"*Non*," said Du Pré, "he will be back."

"Before she kills herself maybe," said Madelaine.

Du Pré patted Madelaine on the leg.

"She is strong," said Du Pré. "She rides and rides until she can sleep."

"So smart," said Madelaine, "and now this."

Du Pré nodded.

Pallas had come back from school, her eyes deep in her head, her skin pale, listless, hardly able to eat. She was proud and would not complain, but she was in great pain.

"Bart wants her to go to a hospital," said Du Pré.

"They are not worth a shit," said Madelaine. "Benetsee is though."

Du Pré sighed, nodded, had some more whiskey.

Madelaine fished a bottle of the pink fizzy wine she liked from the soft cooler in the backseat, and she poured a travel mug full. The sweet smell filled the car.

Du Pré had a good fifteen miles of clear road ahead. He got up to speed.

They shot past a parked Highway Patrol car that was hidden in a cleft in the land, behind some flat rocks.

Du Pré honked.

The patrol car flashed its lights.

"That is McPhie," said Du Pré.

"I know it is McPhie," said Madelaine. "They send other cops to do McPhie's job and they stop all the people driving fast and they piss off people so then somebody gets the drop on them, locks them in their trunk, and calls the Highway Patrol, says get this asshole out of here before we shoot him, and then we have McPhie back."

Du Pré laughed.

"Nobody is going to shoot a cop," said Du Pré.

"Maybe," said Madelaine. "But it helps when they think somebody might."

Du Pré grinned. McPhie was a huge man, had played pro football for a while, until injuries slowed him down. He was from here, the plains, and he knew the people. Proud, not fond of *guvverment*, and extremely pugnacious. Very good soldiers came from here.

"We got to do something for Pallas," said Madelaine.

"Yes," said Du Pré.

"You hear me, Du Pré?" said Madelaine.

"Yes," said Du Pré.

"OK," said Madelaine.

· Chapter 2 ·

DU PRÉ SAT ON his buckskin mountain horse, Walkin'
John, looking out over the plains below. He was on a pocket
meadow in the flank of the mountain the trail ran up.

He had followed Pallas's mount's tracks, which had gone
back down another trail.

Then he saw her ride out of the trees below and the horse
began to canter and then to gallop.

Du Pré shook his head.

He turned Walkin' John and they headed down the trail
that Pallas had taken fifteen or so minutes before.

"I won't make you run that hard," said Du Pré to Walkin'
John.

Walkin' John said *whuffie*.

By the time Du Pré came out of the trees below Pallas
had vanished. He rode to a ridge that reached out from the
mountain, got down, dropped the reins on the ground, and
walked to a spur of rock with a hundred-foot drop below it.

Pallas was a couple of miles away, cantering up a switchback trail. She would get to the top and probably go east, Du
Pré thought.

He rode Walkin' John down a ridge trail that dropped to

a hill, went along the crest, and then he crossed the arroyo on a bench of yellow-gray rock that would be a waterfall if there was more water.

He wound down to a small creek, along its banks, up a hill.

Pallas came out of a stand of aspens.

She saw Du Pré, rode up to him.

Her face was flushed from the wind and sun.

"Hello, Granpère," she said.

"How is the horse?" said Du Pré.

"Stewball is a good horse," she said, "too old to race him now. You remember that?"

Du Pré nodded.

Right-wing nuts, bush races, a lot of money, a lot of death.

But Pallas and Lourdes had each gotten a very good horse out of it.

"You are riding after me," said Pallas. "Madelaine is worried. I am getting through the day and then I have the night, Granpère."

Du Pré nodded.

"I am doing what I can," said Pallas. "Bart is ver' sweet, he wants to send me to a hospital. I tell him will they give me a new heart? I think my heart is dead, Granpère . . ."

"Bart tries to help," said Du Pré.

A squirrel chirred, scolding an intruder off in the lodgepole forest that covered the flanks of the mountain. Then another.

Du Pré and Pallas turned.

"Bear, maybe?" said Pallas.

Du Pré shrugged.

"Maybe," he said.

They waited.

Then one of the golden eagles that lived on the sheer cliff to the west flew down. The huge bird circled once and then rose up, wings pumping slowly.

Benetsee trotted out of the timber.

He was black with dirt, his running shoes were torn, he wore a headband that might have once been red.

The old man looked at Du Pré and Pallas, waved once, and he then vanished into a little watercourse that ran away from them.

"I am going to shoot him," said Du Pré.

"You been going, shoot him, since I am old enough to hear," said Pallas. "But so far? You don't shoot him."

"I miss a few times," said Du Pré.

A coyote trotted out of the ground, it was there one moment where there had been nothing before.

The coyote disappeared into yellow grass.

Then Benetsee came trotting up the trail.

Du Pré looked at the big rock the old man had been behind.

Benetsee stopped, grinned.

"Old man," said Du Pré, "Madelaine see you, you get *boiled*."

"She is a kind woman," said Benetsee, "ver' kind."

Du Pré fished a flask out of the saddlebag, he took off the top, handed it to the old man.

Benetsee emptied it.

. . . Water, wine, whiskey, beer, old bastard drinks them all same way, right on down, like that . . . Du Pré thought.

"Ah," said Benetsee, "now I am numb, maybe go see Madelaine, take a bath."

He slid up behind Du Pré.

"You got bugs?" said Du Pré.

"Big ones," said Benetsee, "tired of old me, they are piling on you now. Lots of them too. They will have a good time . . ."

They rode down the hill.

"I think I ride some more," said Pallas.

"*Non*," said Benetsee sharply, "horse, you come on." He said something in an old language. Stewball pricked up his ears and followed, ignoring Pallas and her jerks on the reins.

"I don't want to trouble anyone," said Pallas.

"And you stay on the damn horse," said Benetsee.

Pallas stuck her right boot back in the stirrup.

She slumped in the saddle.

"I'm sorry," she said.

Benetsee turned to look back at her.

"You got nothing to be sorry for," he said, "you need good tea, a sweat, water from Skull Springs."

"It tastes terrible," said Pallas.

Benetsee laughed.

"You do as I say," he said. "I got lots, worry about, don't got to worry about you too. I help you, Madelaine don't kick my ass . . ."

Pallas laughed, though tears were streaming down her cheeks.

"It is not just your life, here," said Benetsee, "mine too."

"Madelaine is not going to kill you," said Pallas.

"No," said Benetsee, "but she make me suffer so much I do it."

Du Pré laughed.

They came into the huge pasture above Bart's house. Du Pré had opened the gate, and Pallas rode Stewball through it.

"Where is Moondog?" said Du Pré.

"Split hoof," said Pallas. "Lourdes, she take him to Sam, get the hoof taken care of."

"You give him cottonseed cake?" said Benetsee.

"No, we give him that stuff Bart buys," said Pallas, "supposed to be good for hooves, hair, teeth."

"Bart don't know horses," said Benetsee.

"Booger Tom does," said Pallas.

"Yah," said Benetsee.

"Booger Tom has been hollering for cottonseed cake," said Pallas.

"Bart don't think nothing is good unless it is expensive," said Benetsee.

They passed Bart's house, went to the county road, then through another gate into another huge pasture.

The little town of Toussaint was nine miles away.

They cantered most of the distance, rode to the small pasture that sat behind Madelaine's house.

Du Pré looked at the sky, clear, no rain coming.

"I should take Stewball to the barn," said Pallas.

She tried to turn the big horse but he wouldn't budge.

A huge dog came out of the willows. The animal just appeared. It was white with caramel-brown patches on its body and one caramel ear. Its tail had been docked.

The huge dog trotted up to Pallas, who was stripping the saddle and blanket and reins and bit from Stewball. She looked down at the dog.

"Hello," said Pallas to the dog.

The huge dog sat, its head cocked.

Pallas patted the big head.

"You know this dog?" said Du Pré.

"No," said Pallas, "he is a good big dog though. Wonder what kind of dog."

"Some kind of dog," said Du Pré.

The big dog stood up, looked at Pallas again, and then trotted to the line of willows by the little creek and was gone.

· Chapter 3 ·

DU PRÉ WATCHED THE fire rise and begin to heat the stones, set on ricks of wood split small, so it would ignite quickly. The flames curled around the stones, worn round quartzite, tight in the grain and able to take heat without cracking.

He walked down to the creek behind Benetsee's cabin, looked in the long pool that had the waving water plants and the little brook trout hiding in the trailing green leaves. The bottom was gold, dappled by the sun.

Madelaine and Pallas and Benetsee sat at the plank table Du Pré had made for the old man many years ago. The table was worn and gray now; the sun and the winter had stained it a soft silver.

Benetsee was wearing brand-new clothes and running shoes with fabric ties, Velcro straps that ran over the arch. The shoes were bright blue and had panels of reflective silver on the sides.

The old man had a new headband, bright red, and a vest of soft doeskin painted with a few symbols, sun and eagle, shield and lance, a stone knife and a prickly pear cactus.

He was a few shades lighter. The soot from the campfires had been scrubbed away and his lank white hair was braided and gathered with straps of otter fur.

. . . I ran over that damn otter . . . Du Pré thought . . . dumb bastard was crossing the road for some reason, long damn way from where any otter should be . . .

The fire under the stones crackled, and then the first of the ricks collapsed and the stone sank down on hot red coals. The others fell one by one, and the stones started to look white, and heat shimmered above them.

Pallas drank from a plastic milk jug. Her face screwed up.

"This tastes like goat piss," she said, "sorry-ass goat piss." Benetsee grinned.

"Got a whole jug to go," he said, "all that goat piss, you are ver' lucky woman."

Pallas drank more. Madelaine patted her hand.

"I am fine now," said Pallas. "I stuck my finger, the electric outlet, everything better."

"She is bitching," said Madelaine. "That is a good sign."

Pallas took another long draft of the water. "Yuck," she said.

Du Pré laughed. He took a steel-handled shovel and he pushed the blade under a stone and he carried it to the sweat lodge and he put it in the stone pit. He carried seven others there.

He filled a small bucket with creek water, and he put a battered blue enamel dipper in the bucket. Du Pré waited.

He looked toward the mountains.

Pallas stripped on the big towel beside Du Pré and she crawled into the lodge. Du Pré did not look at her.

"OK," said Pallas. She dribbled water on the stones and the hot rocks turned the water to steam.

Du Pré flipped the thick blankets down over the entrance. The hissing was muffled but it was still loud. He walked back to the table.

"You two go up, front porch," said Benetsee. Madelaine got up and she and Du Pré walked up the hill to the cabin and around it. There was a small narrow front porch with one bench on it; the top lifted up so kindling could be stored in the box beneath.

Benetsee began to sing, his old voice rich and strong, vast for so small a man. Drumming.

"I am scraping the dirt off that old goat," said Madelaine, "got the brush I use for the carpet so he bleeds some, old bastard, and he is laughing. I am cussing him, staying away for a long time, he said he comes when he needs to, can't do much until the heart is ready. That poor girl, I am afraid for weeks she will jump off a cliff, go into the rocks, we find her broken there."

Du Pré nodded.

"Bart is ready, roll her up in a rug, fly her to Switzerland," said Madelaine. "I have to grab him, shake, say Pallas has to be here, her people are here."

Du Pré nodded.

"Skull Springs water," said Madelaine, "stuff bubbles and fizzes."

Du Pré nodded.

"Mineral water," he said, "has lithium in it."

"Stuff they give nutcases?" said Madelaine.

"Some nutcases," said Du Pré. "Whites, they build those big hotels near springs like Skull Springs, so people can drink the water, sit around, and bitch."

Madelaine laughed.

"Like that place over, the Boulder River." she said.

"Yah," said Du Pré.

An old hotel. Now in the summer there were camps there where white women from big cities came to listen to people who waved rattles and who painted their faces and chanted in strange tongues. They offered "vision quests," too, for thousands of dollars, visions guaranteed.

Madelaine bumped Du Pré. He nodded and he rolled a smoke and then lit it. He handed the cigarette to Madelaine.

"Make another, yourself," she said. "I want all this this time." He rolled another.

The singing and drumming got louder, more voices seemed to have joined in, more sticks on the drum.

Du Pré saw movement out of the corner of his eye, and he turned and looked off to the west.

The big white-and-caramel dog was there, looking at him. The dog padded past the west side of the cabin.

"What is that dog?" said Madelaine. "It does not look like an accidental dog."

"I don't know and no, it does not," said Du Pré. The singing and drumming had stopped.

Du Pré and Madelaine got up and they walked down the slope to the little flat where the sweat lodge was.

Pallas's head was above the water in the long pool, Benetsee was not in sight.

The huge dog sat by the pool, looking at Pallas.

Du Pré sat on an old stump, Madelaine took a fresh towel, a big one, down by the creek and she handed it to Pallas when the girl slipped up out of the water.

Pallas dried herself, then she stood on the towel and Madelaine handed her clothing, all fresh and clean.

Du Pré looked off to the north, where the Wolf Mountains rose up blue and gray and white. The two golden eagles were riding the updrafts, wings set, passing each other and going on.

Pallas toweled her long thick black hair.

"You are one big dog," said Pallas to the still beast, patting his huge head.

The big dog stood up, looking off toward the mountains. He seemed to have heard something.

Du Pré saw a man in camouflage trotting along a hilltop. The man stopped and put field glasses to his eyes. He was perhaps two miles away.

The huge dog leaped over the creek at the foot of the pool where it narrowed and went through the willows and cottonwoods on the far side.

The dog ran fast; a coyote leaped up out of a cleft in the earth and it ran pell-mell away from the big dog, which did not notice it.

The white-and-caramel dog disappeared, swallowed by the land.

Then it appeared again.

It raced up the hill where the man in the camouflage stood and when the big dog got to the man it rose up and put paws on the man's shoulders.

Du Pré watched the two walk toward Bart's. . . . Now what has he got himself into? . . . Du Pré thought.

"I am ver' tired," said Pallas. "I am ver' tired."

She looked ready to fall.

Du Pré just picked her up and he carried her to the old cruiser and he handed her to Madelaine, who was in the backseat.

They drove to Madelaine's, and Du Pré carried his granddaughter in to the house and he put her on a bed. He went out of the room while Madelaine undressed her and put her under the covers.

Benetsee had disappeared.

Du Pré went outside. The huge dog was on the porch.

He looked at Du Pré.

"Good evening," said Du Pré.

· **Chapter 4** ·

DU PRÉ ATE THE last bite of his cheeseburger and he drank the last three inches of his ditchwater highball.

"How's Pallas?" said Susan Klein. Her husband, Benny, was the sheriff and Susan had quit teaching school to run the saloon. It was just like a classroom full of cranky eight-year-olds so she felt right at home. Du Pré shrugged. "Benetsee came," he said, "they sweat, he has her drinking Skull Springs water."

"Good," said Susan Klein. "That fixed my mom, you know." Du Pré looked at her.

"People here got the blues," said Susan, "they'd drink Skull Springs water, and they'd feel better. Lithium."

Du Pré nodded.

The front door opened and a gust of cool evening air punched through the cigarette smoke and booze fumes.

Du Pré turned his head, saw Bart and Pidgeon enter with another man, a tall fellow with a black mustache and a high, round-collared shirt that had silver embroidery on a dark blue fabric.

He wore high boots of soft brown leather.

Du Pré nodded. The man walked on the balls of his feet, set wide. A horseman.

The three came up to Du Pré.

"Du Pré," said Bart, "this is Idries Arghanov." Du Pré stood, put out his hand. "Met your dog," he said.

Pidgeon laughed. She was so beautiful men stared at her, and her rich booming laugh made people smile, even if they didn't know what was funny.

Idries grinned.

"Berkut," he said, "seems to feel your granddaughter needs him."

"Berkut," said Du Pré. "So you are not from Chicago." They all laughed.

"Madelaine coming?" said Pidgeon.

Du Pré shook his head. "She is watching Pallas," he said.

"Well," said Pidgeon, "I will go and watch Pallas too."

"Berkut is there, too, watching," said Idries. "If he wants to stay I hope that that is all right."

"That is some kind of dog," said Du Pré.

"He's a Tobet," said Idries. "They have guarded our camps and herds for thousands of years."

Du Pré looked at Bart. "Let's get a table," said Bart, cheerfully.

. . . Now what . . . Du Pré thought.

They went to a table set in an alcove off the dance floor. It was fairly private and choked sounds off.

"Idries is a Kazakh," said Bart, as they seated themselves.

"Bart buy a ranch in Kazakhstan?" said Du Pré.

Idries looked at Du Pré. His black eyes were twinkling. "Camels," he said.

"No camels" said Du Pré. "I am not going there to herd camels."

"If you could just shut the fuck up for two minutes," said Bart, "I will let you know what Idries is here for."

"He is here," said Du Pré, "because he lives in a very bad neighborhood which has lots of oil and good old Bart here is helping with the Neighborhood Watch."

"Quite right," said Idries. A cell phone chirred in his pocket and he nodded apologetically and got up and went out the front door.

Bart looked at Du Pré. His worn red face broke into a grin. "I don't know why I bother trying to explain things to you," he said. "You seem to know before I can say anything."

"It is not hard," said Du Pré. "Kazakhstan is a very long way off and that man is a soldier and Kazakhstan looks a lot like Montana so I think he is here for that reason, too, so there are others or there will be others."

Bart nodded. "OK," he said.

"The dogs," said Du Pré.

"The Tobets," said Bart. "Samantha and I are going to raise Tobets and train them."

Du Pré felt another puff of wind.

Idries was coming toward them, and he was chattering away in French with Father Van Den Heuvel. The big clumsy priest was smiling.

Du Pré got up to let Idries and Father Van Den Heuvel sit in the back on the bench set against the wall.

Father Van Den Heuvel spoke either Bulgarian or Gaelic and Idries laughed.

Du Pré looked at the big priest.

"I'm so glad you have someone to talk to," said Du Pré.

"He even talks English," said Booger Tom, who had also come in and was standing behind Du Pré.

The old cowboy found a chair and slid it over.

"Let's get a bigger table," said Booger Tom, "since we seem to be havin' one of them United Nations meetin's."

They went to the big round table.

Benetsee came out of the back, where the johns were. The old man shuffled over to the big round table and he sat across from Idries. Bart made introductions.

Benetsee grinned.

Susan Klein came with a beer schooner filled with cheap white wine and she set it in front of the old man, and she set ditchwater highballs in front of Du Pré and Booger Tom, brandy in front of Father Van Den Heuvel, and two glasses of club soda with lime in front of Bart and Idries.

. . . Muslim . . . Du Pré thought.

Idries looked at Du Pré. "No pork, no alcohol," he said. "Mohammed was a wise man."

"Yes," said Du Pré, drinking from his ditch.

"No ham and no whiskey," said Booger Tom. "I am so glad I am a good Christian."

"Christ," said Father Van Den Heuvel, "don't start that crap with me, you miserable old bastard."

"He has buttons," said Booger Tom, "right there on the front of that tussock or whatever he calls it."

"A cassock," said Father Van Den Heuvel, "has been in style among Jesuits since your ancestors were being hanged for petty theft."

"Not petty," said Booger Tom. "We was never petty."

Susan Klein set down a big platter of meats and cheeses and peppers and green onions and crackers. "That's beef salami, mixed with deer," she said, looking at Idries.

Idries smiled. "Thank you," he said.

"We made it here," said Susan. "No mystery meats from hell."

They all laughed.

. . . I am not going to fucking Kazakhstan . . . Du Pré thought.

Benetsee had sat silently, quaffing his mighty mug of bad white wine.

Then he said something, looking at Idries. Du Pré didn't know the language; it was one Benetsee chanted sometimes when he was in the sweat lodge, singing to the past.

Idries looked startled.

Benetsee repeated himself.

Idries looked down at the table. Then he replied, some-what haltingly.

Benetsee said something else.

Idries looked at him and replied, again rather slowly. The man was having to search for the words in his mind.

Father Van Den Heuvel was staring from one man to the other.

Benetsee got up, he nodded, and he said something to Idries and Idries got up and they walked toward the front door. Father Van Den Heuvel was smiling, looking into his snifter.

"Somebody like to tell us fools what the hell's goin' on?" said Booger Tom.

"I think," said the big priest, slowly, "that Idries and Benet-see are conversing in a very ancient tongue."

Du Pré looked at him.

"Benetsee knows it," said Father Van Den Heuvel, "and Idries knows it, so what we just listened to was a first conver-sation in perhaps eight or ten thousand years . . ."

Du Pré nodded.

"I imagine that if you checked Benetsee's DNA against Idries's," said Father van den Heuvel, "they would be quite closely related."

Du Pré nodded.

. . . Long time gone, very long, but the language changes very slowly . . .

· Chapter 5 ·

PALLAS AND THE huge white-and-caramel dog were sitting out behind Madelaine's under a lilac bush that was a good fifteen feet high and thick with Persian double-white blooms.

Madelaine's backyard was filled with lilacs, several kinds, and flowers set in raised beds, even a small pond that had cattails. The pond was a spring, and though it was only three feet or so across, it carried enough water to flush the algae out before it could bloom. A single big fat toad lived near the spring.

Du Pré sat down across from the two women.

Berkut was alert, looking around for any danger.

"It was so nice of Idries to give him to me," said Pallas. "Berkut is one great dog."

Du Pré nodded.

Idries had come, found Berkut and Pallas together, and he had said something to the big dog. The Tobet had barked once, Idries had nodded.

"He has decided his place is with you," he said to Pallas. "If you will keep him, that is what he wants."

"You bet," said Pallas, smiling. She was really smiling, and she had not done that much for a very long time.

"How is the goat piss?" said Du Pré, pointing to one of the jugs of Skull Springs water.

"Goat piss," said Pallas. "But I put some cranberry juice in it, it is fruity goat piss, which is some better."

Du Pré inhaled. The scent of lilacs was thick and sweet. Bees were feeding on the blossoms, and so were some small hummingbirds, flying jewels.

Du Pré yawned.

"You are tired, Granpère," said Pallas. "You go sleep."

"*Non*," said Du Pré, "I am just old. Pret' soon I sleep for a ver' long time."

Pallas laughed.

Du Pré got up.

"I have to go, Bart's," he said.

"Give my best to them, say hi to Idries. Tell him he can't have Berkut back," said Pallas, "he's my guy."

Du Pré laughed.

Madelaine opened the screen door.

"Du Pré!" she said. "That Jack La Salle is on the telephone."

Du Pré nodded.

He walked into the kitchen, picked up the telephone.

"General," said Du Pré.

"Retired," said La Salle. "I always hoped to be known as Jack, or La Salle, or hey asshole, rather than general. I did the general bit. I tried to do it well. Now why don't you fucking well quit pulling my dick because I've told you this before."

"OK," said Du Pré.

"And I need a favor," said La Salle.

"Sure," said Du Pré.

. . . My friend sounds troubled and ver' angry . . .

"You remember the mess at the prison in Afghanistan?" said La Salle. "Well, the soldier who turned in those 'advisers' had to be guarded round the clock. There were all sorts of people who swore to kill him. For doing the right thing, for Chrissakes. The foremost being that demented billionaire

Lloyd Cutler who owns Temple Security from which the hired advisers come. Cutler makes his money on sweetheart contracts with the government, and he gets those because he gives millions to politicians. Lately he's found Jesus, who he talks to, I suspect, often, and now he's recruiting the worst of the Christer loons, at least those who have very thorough military training, for his private security company. Thinks he's doing God's work."

"So you want to send the soldier whistleblower here because now that the trials are over he gets no protection anymore," said Du Pré. "They don't have the money, had to give rich folks all those tax breaks."

"It's worse than that," said La Salle. "There are plenty of people besides Cutler in this sewer who actively want him dead. God, how I love Washington, DC."

"I will talk to Bart," said Du Pré. "But you send him now because Bart will say yes of course."

"Fine," said La Salle. "You should also know that there are a few Special Forces guys training out your way too. I am not supposed to know about it but, well, I have some good friends who also want to see this guy make it. And I'll know more about it all shortly. So I'll know more about them shortly."

"OK," said Du Pré.

"Thanks," said La Salle.

"Who is this man?" said Du Pré.

"His name is Hoyt Poe, he's from some dusty little Texas town, and the simple son of a bitch loves mom, apple pie, and the American flag, and felt he owed his country his service and his loyalty. Now, Hoyt is not the most brilliant of men, so he actually believed that the army was an honorable organization, that the laws should be obeyed, and it was in addition just plain wrong to be torturing people. He's deeply religious. So's his wife," said La Salle. "Hoyt's father was killed in Afghanistan in 2011 and so Hoyt joined up as soon as he could, three years ago. He's just a soldier, but a good one."

"What about these Special Forces guys, are here?" said Du Pré.

"I'll call you," said La Salle.

"I will be at Bart's," said Du Pré. "Call there, I have to see this Kazakh about a dog."

"Yes," said La Salle, "good old Bart. You know, the war effort in the Second World War ran quite smoothly because of people like Bart's grandfather. They saw to it that the unions behaved, no one got too greedy, and that the trains ran on time . . ."

Du Pré hung up the telephone.

Madelaine looked at him.

"Guy testified in that Afghanistan prison torture case, those bad people got sentenced," said Du Pré, "same people are trying to kill him."

"Goddamn," said Madelaine. She almost never had goddamning anything so she was good and mad.

"He is coming here," said Du Pré, "with his wife and little girl."

"For doing the right thing," said Madelaine.

"Yah," said Du Pré.

Madelaine smiled, then she grinned.

"OK," she said.

Du Pré looked at her.

"Du Pré," she said, "this general calls you when he needs something done right."

"He is a ver' desperate man," said Du Pré.

"Yah," said Madelaine, then "Pallas is better I think."

"Benetsee is around," said Du Pré.

"He will be here for a while," said Madelaine. "That Idries has a grandfather who is coming here, see Benetsee."

Du Pré looked at her. "Oh," he said.

Information went from Pidgeon to Madelaine at something a good deal faster than the speed of light.

"When?" said Du Pré.

"Soon," said Madelaine. "This old man has to have a passport. He speaks whatever Kazakhs live in the mountains speak. Idries can't go and get him, though."

Du Pré nodded.

"You know Bart has a plane can fly from here to Hong Kong without stopping for gas?" said Madelaine.

"Not from here," said Du Pré, "maybe from Billings."

"So you got to take Booger Tom there," said Madelaine.

"Booger Tom has a passport?" said Du Pré.

"I guess," said Madelaine.

Du Pré laughed.

"He has a *name?*" said Du Pré. "One that did not make the computer spit out a thousand old warrants?"

"He has a name," said Madelaine.

"My head is hurting," said Du Pré.

"Fine," said Madelaine, "but Bart wants you to take Booger Tom and him to Billings."

"They can both drive," said Du Pré. "I was just in Billings listening to some child tell me I don't have bad cancer. A child who should be hitting puberty next year."

"Du Pré," said Madelaine, "you know what that old man they are going to get means, yes?"

Du Pré nodded. "Goddamned right I do," he said. "It means I got three miserable old farts I got to put up with. Three old bastards on my ass now. I am so happy I could puke."

Madelaine laughed. "Maybe you get some luck," she said, "maybe this one is not an old bastard like Booger Tom and Benetsee."

"If he was not," said Du Pré, "they would not be going to get him."

"The poor Du Pré," said Madelaine. "It is hard for him."

"I will be picking up the Poes and bringing them back here is why I am going," said Du Pré. "Why they don't just tell me that? I am not supposed to know until the very last minute?"

Madelaine nodded.

"Oh, they are trying to be careful," she said.

"I wish that they were better at it," said Du Pré.

· Chapter 6 ·

BART SAT IN the shotgun seat and Booger Tom was in the
back, his worn boots on the windowsill. It was warm and the
wind was filled with the scent of clover.

Booger Tom had his hat over his face. . . . That old wolf is
not sleeping . . . Du Pre thought.

"Hoyt Poe," said Bart.

Du Pré nodded. He rolled a smoke with his right hand
while he steered with the left.

"It's not right," said Bart, glaring at Du Pré's cigarette. Du
Pré pushed the lighter in and he waited and when it popped
out he touched it to the end of the cigarette. "Because he does
the right thing, he has to hide out in the middle of nowhere.
He came from the middle of nowhere but at least it didn't
have a lot of snow," said Bart. "What is this country coming
to?"

"Don't get me started on the guvverment," said Booger
Tom from under his hat.

"This old bastard really has a *passport*?" said Du Pré.

"Yup," said Booger Tom, "I even got a couple of credit
cards. Hell, I even joined the AARP."

"I cannot stand this," said Du Pré.

"And you are going to Kazakhstan to pick up some other old goat," said Du Pré, "there will be three of you. Three of you to make my life hell."

"It only takes one and part-time at that," said Booger Tom from under his hat, "you bein' such a sensitive soul and given to tantrums."

"It's my fault," said Bart. "Idries was talking about Benetsee and about this old fart in Kazakhstan who is his grandfather or something and Idries was going on about how wonderful it would be for those two old guys to meet and Samantha said of course it could be arranged. And I of course agreed."

"Ya know," said Booger Tom, crawling out from under his hat, "it's bad enough Pidgeon is about the most gorgeous woman on earth without she has to be smart too. Other'n marryin' Bart, which lapse makes no sense at all whatever."

"You've never seen me naked," said Bart.

"God is merciful," said Booger Tom, "an' I am actually lookin' forward to meetin' this feller. Mukhtar Khan."

"Mukhtar Khan," said Du Pré.

"I wonder if he has a passport yet," said Bart.

"I don't expect any trouble with customs," said Booger Tom. "I hear ol' Mukhtar never goes anywhere without a couple bandoliers of rifle cartridges and his trusty Kalashnikov. I seen a picture of him. He looks like an old bandit. A real prosperous old bandit."

"When you were making those beautiful horsehair ropes, there in Deer Lodge," said Du Pré, "what were you in for?"

"I was such a famed rope maker," said Booger Tom, "the governor stuck me in there. A state treasure, he sez and he give me a nice paper and all, and after I finished the rope he wanted they said they'd let me out. Took a little time, as it was a long rope."

"What were you in for?" said Du Pré.

"Manslaughter," said Booger Tom. "The three of them was no loss, and in fact they really needed killin', so I only had the one charge and did m' thirty months."

"Who was this?" said Bart.

"Three of those no-account Walkers from up the northwest," said Booger Tom.

"What was the argument about?" said Bart.

"No argument," said Booger Tom. "I knowed they was plannin' to kill me and I just beat them to it."

"How did you know they were planning to kill you?" said Bart, "and over what, for God's sakes?"

"You know how them people are," said Booger Tom, "and you are gettin' awful nosy."

"Christ," said Bart.

Booger Tom lifted up his old Peacemaker, and he looked at the cylinder.

"For Chrissakes," said Bart, "you are not taking that fucking thing to Kazakhstan."

"I hear it is a dangerous place," said Booger Tom.

"Stop the car," said Bart, "and we'll throw him out."

Du Pré nodded and he speeded up.

"I thought you was somebody," said Booger Tom. "You'd deprive a pore old man of his shootin' arn?"

"Just quit fucking with me," said Bart, "it gives me migraines."

Booger Tom grinned.

"I'll leave the gun," he said. "And the three Walkers was stealing some cattle a place I was ridin' for and I come on 'em and things got out of hand sort of and you know how it is when things gets out of hand. I was in some of a hurry, as there was three of them and one of me and the judge said it was sorta excessive, me killin' all three. So I rare up on m' hind legs and tell that sorry son of a bitch ta shove his little wooden hammer up his ass as he was not there and I was and what the hell is he thinkin' givin' me advice in a matter like that. I added he was a fat dumb son of a bitch who prolly never killed nobody so where the hell he gets so expert in such matters I purely cannot see . . ."

"Oh," said Bart, "you got thirty months for shooting off your damned mouth."

"I suppose," said Booger Tom.

"Either that," Booger Tom added, "or maybe I got it because the stupid bastard I had for a lawyer was tryin' to pull me back down in the chair and so I sorta hit him to make him stop."

"What did you hit him with?" said Bart.

"Well," said Booger Tom, "the chair, of course, on account it seemed so important to him. It was one of them heavy oak ones they favor in courthouses."

"Did the attorney live?" said Bart.

"Sure did," said Booger Tom. "He got most of his motor control back over time. Least I heard that."

"I wish," said Bart, "they had just hung you."

"Then the governor wouldn't have got no rope," said Booger Tom. "You see, it makes sense if you think it all the way through."

Du Pré slowed and he turned on the ramp that went to the expressway and he pulled in behind a big semitrailer and then he went around it. There was not much traffic.

"Do you believe any of what that lying old bastard just said?" said Bart, looking at Du Pré.

"*Non*," said Du Pré.

"I thought so," said Bart. "I wonder if any of it is true."

"It's true," said Booger Tom, "there was a sort of scuffle then, you know, them bailiffs jumped me on account of I was plannin' to wrap what was left of the chair around the judge's head. All of this crap come of me doin' such a fine public service as to get rid of three of them dumb Walker bastards. Don't get me started on the guvverment . . ."

Du Pré had some whiskey. He rolled another smoke.

They rode in silence clear to the Billings airport, and Du Pré went to the gate that led to the private plane hangars.

He stopped the big green SUV next to a jet aircraft, medium in size, with long wings and a graceful shape. The door started to fold out and down. Steps appeared.

A customs agent walked over.

Booger Tom and Bart got out, the customs agent glanced at their bags and them and he signed off on the forms. Booger Tom grinned at Du Pré. He held up his hogleg.

Bart threw up his hands and he pointed at the steps while he yelled at Booger Tom. Du Pré couldn't hear anything because the jet's engines were gathering force. Bart walked over to Du Pré. He handed Du Pré a slip of paper.

"The Poes are at this motel," said Bart. "Their possessions are coming by truck. But they are at that address . . ."

Du Pré looked at the paper.

"You know where that is?" said Bart.

Du Pré nodded.

"There are a couple of security men there, military," said Bart. "They are expecting you."

Du Pré nodded.

"They said not to tell you until we got here," said Bart.

"You could have driven," said Du Pré, "so this was pretty dumb. I knew this was probably why."

"Tell them that," said Bart.

Du Pré shook his head. "No," he said, "I don't think I will bother."

Bart went up the steps of the jet and the door lifted and shut. The plane turned slowly and crept toward the runway.

Du Pré got in the SUV. He had another drink of whiskey.

. . . Old bastards will be my own plague . . . now . . . three of them . . .

· **Chapter 7** ·

THE MOTEL WAS an old one, brick, and the rooms could be rented by the day or the week or the month. A sign on the desk said that dogs were allowed but could not be left in the rooms unattended.

Du Pré waited until a fat man in a soiled T-shirt came out of the back. He looked at Du Pré.

"I am here for some people," he said. "Tell them Du Pré is here."

The fat man looked at Du Pré, nodded, picked up the telephone, punched some numbers.

Then he went back, without a word.

Du Pré waited outside, smoking a cigarette.

A door opened and a big square-built man in a suit that looked too small for him came out. His thick arms strained the fabric. His neck was almost wider than his head. He walked toward Du Pré, arms swinging.

Du Pré looked at him.

The man came up close.

"ID," he said.

Du Pré took out his wallet, flipped it open, held it up.

The man looked at the driver's license. "La Salle said it

was OK," he said, "and if he says so it is. Now we got the Poes up here and we want them safe. We can go along with you to Toussaint . . ."

Du Pré nodded. "I thank you, but I think it will be all right," he said. "You got them out without anyone knowing, right?"

"Dead of night," said the man.

"So if you were not followed," said Du Pré, "and if they have no other way of knowing where you went, it will be OK for some time."

The big man nodded. "You armed?" he said.

Du Pré nodded.

"Wheel that SUV over and we'll get them in," said the man. "Those poor kids. Christ, Poe turns in criminals, and now he and his family are on the run. This business makes me sick . . ."

Du Pré drove over to the room. The green SUV had heavily tinted windows, and Du Pré opened all the doors.

Hoyt and Sandra and Faith Helen Poe came out in a rush, blinking. The sun was bright. They got in the backseat.

The men guarding them carried suitcases out and a bag of toys for the little girl, and a small cooler.

The Poes were in shorts and T-shirts and rubber sandals.

The men shut the doors.

The big man held out his hand.

"La Salle sends his best," he said. They shook hands once.

"You give him mine," said Du Pré. He got in the SUV, backed, turned, drove out and down the street and to an on-ramp. They were soon outside of Billings. Du Pré looked in the rearview mirror.

"You want music or anything?" he said.

"Oh, no, mister," said Sandra, "We're pretty tired. It's a little cold, though."

"There are blankets in the back," said Du Pré, "and pillows. There is pop and food in the soft cooler."

Hoyt Poe was a crew-cut blond young man with a broad open face.

Sandra Poe was a pretty girl, slender, with thick blond hair that was gathered in a single braid.

Little Faith Helen was a white-haired child, pale of skin, with enormous blue eyes that were tired and grave.

The child was scared and needed a home and people who she could trust.

"There is a little bed back there," said Du Pré, "if the little girl needs to sleep."

Du Pré rolled a smoke, lit it, opened the window.

Sandra glared at him.

But she didn't say anything.

Du Pré grinned. He had another pull of whiskey.

"Oh, Lord," said Sandra, "you're drinking, too."

"There is beer and wine in the cooler," said Du Pré.

Sandra flushed, started to say something. Hoyt patted her knee and he grinned and then she laughed.

"I'm sorry," she said, "we're tired and we're scared."

"It will be all right, honey," said Hoyt. His drawl was thick, Southern, liquid.

Sandra began to weep, then she wiped her face and she smiled.

"It's good of you people to take us in," she said. "We've been living like we're the criminals. We've been moved from place to place."

"I am sorry," said Du Pré.

Hoyt smiled. "Mountains where we're goin'?" he said.

"Yes," said Du Pré, "ver' good mountains."

"Elk?" said Hoyt. "I always wanted to shoot an elk."

"We will make sure you shoot an elk," said Du Pré. "It is a while until the hunting season."

"This place is called what?" said Hoyt.

"Toussaint," said Du Pré.

"Not very big?" said Hoyt.

"No," said Du Pré.

"Place we come from wasn't big either," he said. "We like little towns."

"We've known each other since we were four," said Sandra.

Du Pré nodded.

Little Faith Helen got restless. Sandra lifted her over the seat and the little girl found the toy bag.

She squealed with delight.

"You can play a little, honey," said Sandra, "then you need a nap."

"Don't want a nap," said Faith Helen.

Du Pré grinned. . . . Talking back already, that is a good sign . . .

"Cattle country," said Hoyt. "I ride pretty good. Haven't for a while though."

He lifted his left arm and he rubbed his shoulder.

Du Pré could see a red welt of new flesh on his arm.

Wounded.

"Fishing?" said Hoyt.

"Sure," said Du Pré.

"Trout?" said Hoyt. "I never caught a trout."

"Trout," said Du Pré.

Sandra had crawled over in back with the little girl. Hoyt leaned forward. "Will they be safe there?" he said.

"Sure," said Du Pré, "it is a long way from anything and we watch who comes."

"They were going to give us new names and all," he said. "But I said no. Poe is an old name, lots of old soldiers, and I didn't want to have to hide in my own country under another name. It didn't seem right . . ."

Du Pré nodded.

"How much you know about us?" said Hoyt.

"You testified against those bastards were torturing people," said Du Pré, "now you got people here want you dead."

"It's hard," said Hoyt. "I joined up right out of high school. At eighteen. Did three tours in Afghanistan and Iraq. Wounded four times. Then I turn in some criminals and I have to go on the run."

"It is hard," said Du Pré.

"Who is General La Salle?" said Hoyt. "I never heard of him, don't know what he does."

"He is a good man," said Du Pré. "He is retired now."

"For a retired general, " said Hoyt, "lots of people jump when he says so, I noticed."

Du Pré nodded.

"You got a school there?" said Hoyt.

"Yes," said Du Pré.

"Preschool?" said Hoyt.

"It's a small town with a lot of little kids," said Du Pré.

· Chapter 8 ·

DU PRÉ PULLED UP to Bart and Pidgeon's house. It was not all that large. It sat in a huge grove of fir trees and there were many barns and outbuildings near it; the horse herd was grazing in the big pasture, and Pidgeon's gardens were a blazing riot of colors. She came out smiling.

"Lord," said Hoyt, "this is some place, ain't it."

Du Pré helped Sandra with the things. Little Faith Helen woke up, rubbed her knuckles in her eyes, and scampered out of the back and to the ground, eager to see the new things.

"Faith Helen!" said Hoyt. "You come on here now."

Pidgeon introduced herself and while she bent down to meet the little girl, Du Pré saw the look Sandra gave her; all women did, Pidgeon was so beautiful she seemed dangerous to them.

"You can stay in the guesthouse until we find a place of your own for you," said Pidgeon. "Come on and we'll get you set."

Du Pré and Hoyt picked up the bags and followed Pidgeon and Sandra and Faith Helen down the narrow drive to the guesthouse, a two-bedroom log house with a long veranda and a swinging porch seat.

The house had a lot of windows and was light and airy. The decor was simple.

Pidgeon showed Sandra the kitchen and Du Pré and Hoyt carried the bags to the master bedroom.

The bed was made up, there were fresh towels on it, books on the nightstands, and fresh flowers in vases all over.

Hoyt laughed.

"Sandra and me grew up in trailers," he said, "like poor folks do. This is pretty rich . . ."

Du Pré nodded, went outside, rolled a smoke, sat on the steps.

Little Faith Helen squealed and yelled, "Dolls!"

Pidgeon came out after a few minutes.

Du Pré stood up.

"Nice kids," said Pidgeon. "Christ, what is happening to them makes me ill. Sandra said the little Texas town they came from had six living generations of her family in it. Now they don't dare go there or even let their people know where they are . . ."

Du Pré and Pidgeon walked back to the main house.

"Bart and Booger Tom take to the air?" she said.

"Yes," said Du Pré, "they go to get Mukhtar Khan. Me, I think I will leave now, go someplace, not tell anyone where I am."

"Too late," said Pidgeon. "Not to mention Madelaine would track you down and kill you."

"Hoyt said he could ride," said Du Pré.

"They need rest first," said Pidgeon. "They have circles under their eyes. When I left they were praying quietly, thanking God for deliverance and asking His help. Good people."

Du Pré nodded.

"Poor people," said Du Pré, "they are supposed to have all their things sent on, but I doubt they own ver' much. He said he enlisted. He has been wounded four times. He reports a very bad crime, and now his own countrymen are trying to kill him for it . . ."

"Not all of his countrymen," said Pidgeon, "are trying to kill him. Some of us are trying to help him. I don't think they had much with them. Do you know when their things will come?"

Du Pré shook his head.

"Maybe La Salle does," said Pidgeon, nodding.

"I need to go to town," said Du Pré, "so do you need anything?"

"I'd like to have my country back," said Pidgeon, "is what I need. This current bunch of assholes are beyond belief."

Du Pré laughed. "Yah," he said.

"But we can do one good thing," said Pidgeon, "so we'll do that."

She kissed Du Pré on the cheek and she turned and walked back to her house.

Du Pré got in his old cruiser and he drove back toward Toussaint. He stopped at a snowplow turnout and he looked down from the benchland to the plains and Toussaint, which looked like it had been dropped into an alien land that didn't like it there and would get rid of it soon enough.

. . . This country, it is just waiting for us to go away . . .

Madelaine was in the saloon, sitting on a high stool behind the bar, peering through her bifocals at the needle in her right hand. The tip of her tongue was stuck in the corner of her mouth.

She jabbed the needle through the thin leather of the pouch she was beading, as well as a small piece of the skin on her left hand.

"Fuck," said Madelaine, a quiet, rather weary comment.

"They got machines do that stuff," said Du Pré. "People to run them; you could save yourself many wounds."

"I am bleeding and you give me crap," said Madelaine. "Guy who loved me, he would be boiling water and getting a tourniquet."

"I love you," said Du Pré, "just I don't see blood."

"You want blood?" said Madelaine. "I show you blood, you Métis son of a bitch."

They kissed, Du Pré leaning far over the bar.

"So they are here," said Madelaine.

"At Bart's," said Du Pré.

"Bart's name is on the papers," said Madelaine, "the place is Pidgeon's."

"I am ver' glad women have the vote," said Du Pré. "I even am no longer mad at my granpère for going off to fight that First World War and letting that happen. It was shellshock and it is over and I am ver' glad of it."

Madelaine nodded. "Fuckin'-A," she said. "You are one happy boy. Now, how are these people? They will be all right here?"

"I don't know," said Du Pré.

"Religious," said Madelaine, "they are from Texas."

"Yes," said Du Pré.

"I don't think they will like Father Van Den Heuvel," said Madelaine. "Probably think Catholics are people of the devil."

"He makes good music," said Du Pré.

Madelaine nodded, pulled a thread through, looked at the bead. She showed the medicine bag to Du Pré.

Tiny beads had been set to a mosaic of a woman wearing a single white feather riding a big roan horse. There was a double sun above her.

"For Pallas?" said Du Pré.

"Yes," said Madelaine. "She is doing some better, that Skull Springs water helps some I think."

Du Pré came round the bar, mixed himself a ditch. He rolled a cigarette and he lit it and he passed it to Madelaine, who took her one drag and handed it back.

"So," said Madelaine, "Pidgeon will bring them here for supper. It is Friday. Turn on the news."

Du Pré pressed the button on the dingus that turned the TV on and off.

He watched for a moment.

"No private jet crashes," he said, "but I still have my hopes."

"Hah," said Madelaine.

Susan Klein bustled in, with two big bags of salad greens she had picked from her garden. She started her lettuces and radishes and scallions early, in a green hothouse, and she canned Italian tomatoes so lightly they were firm enough for salads and fresh garnishes.

A gust of roasting beef smells came out of the kitchen when she opened the door.

"Who are we eating tonight?" said Madelaine.

"Buster," said Susan Klein. "He was real dumb and awful fat. Should be quite good."

All the Angus cattle that were providing the beef for the saloon had names. Susan Klein kept track of their genetic makeup by computer. The beef was always fork-tender and richly flavored. There was a cold trailer out in back where the prime ribs hung for weeks before being cooked.

"May be a busy night," said Madelaine. "You go and see about Pallas now."

Du Pré nodded, finished his drink.

"We got to watch her," said Madelaine.

"I know," said Du Pré.

"She rode over to Benetsee's," said Madelaine.

Du Pré sighed.

"I think I will go on the run," he said.

Madelaine snorted.

Du Pré drove out to Benetsee's cabin.

There were no fires, no one there, not Pallas or Stewball or Berkut the dog.

Du Pré looked up at the Wolf Mountains.

The golden eagles were playing catch-me-if-you-can. The great birds tumbled, swooped, and then they flew up and up and up . . .

· Chapter 9 ·

DU PRÉ HAD GATHERED up four big plastic tubs of soiled dishes and he was hosing them off and stuffing them in the big stainless steel dishwasher. The woman who usually did this was tending a sick child. He wiped his forehead. It was hot and steamy in the kitchen even with the exhaust fan roaring, and the saloon was packed with people.

Friday night was the big night in Toussaint. Saturday was utterly dead.

Madelaine and Jacqueline were carrying platters and big trays out and Susan Klein was doing fourteen things over five cooking stations. She would slice a slab of prime rib, dump one or another sort of potato on it, a garnish of pickled vegetables, and set the platter on the ready shelf with the order clipped above it.

. . . I am lucky to be doing dishes . . . Du Pré thought . . . but I am getting behind. . . . He worked as fast as he could.

The door swung open and a stranger came in, a tall blond man with a thick mustache. He had a tub stacked high with dirty dishes, which he set on the counter where Du Pré pointed.

He grabbed an empty tub and went out and another man, one with a smooth Indio face, and a merry smile, came in with another tub.

"Let me do that," said the Indio, "my fingernails are dirty."

Du Pré laughed and nodded. He rolled a smoke and lit it, offered it to the Mexican man.

"In a minute," he said.

The blond man came back with a tub only half full of dishes. He looked round the kitchen, saw a full garbage can. "Where's that go?" he said, lifting it.

Du Pré opened the back door and he pointed to a big green steel dumpster.

Du Pré smoked while the man lifted the garbage can, very easily, and shook the trash out.

Then he walked back and he grinned at Du Pré.

"I'm Vandevander," he said, "Colonel Richard Vandevander. And I bring you Jack La Salle's best."

Du Pré smiled.

"You are here with Idries," said Du Pré.

"Who," said Vandevander, "is Idries? I never heard of him, but actually he's quite a guy. Started in the Russian Spetsnaz, and when Kazakhstan went independent he made his way home. Speaks eight languages fluently and is a born leader of men . . ."

"Secrets are pret' safe here," said Du Pré, "there is not much of anybody to tell secrets to."

"Yes," said Vandevander, "small town. That other fellow is Master Sergeant Guillermo Sanchez. There are two more, my lieutenant, Chad Chasen, and Sergeant Leroy Mullins."

"I thank you for the help," said Du Pré.

"We came to eat," said Vandevander. "Little R & R, we've been living on grubs and roots for a few days."

. . . They are starving but the first thing they do is help . . . Du Pré thought.

"It should be better, half hour," said Du Pré.

"Odd to find you washing dishes," said Vandevander.

"No," said Du Pré, "when we gave them the vote, that was the end."

Vandevander laughed.

"Men," he said, "are toast. Ah well, we have had a good few thousand years and I seriously doubt women can fuck things up worse 'n we did."

They went back in.

Sanchez had the dishwasher running and he was mopping the floor. All the counters were gleaming clean.

"Mister Sanchez," said Du Pré, "I thank you." He held out his hand and they shook.

"I joined the army," said Sanchez, "so I wouldn't have to do this shit anymore. But, you know, I missed it. I really did. Fingernails are clean too."

Madelaine bustled in.

"There are two guys out on the front porch," she said. "They swept it off and now they are fixing it, those busted places I told you about."

"Oh," said Du Pré.

"You could learn from them," said Madelaine, going back out the door with two impossible armloads of plates.

Du Pré looked at Vandevander who looked at Du Pré.

"Toast," they said.

Sanchez hooted.

"La Salle was right," said Vandevander. "He said Madelaine Placquemines was a born five-star general and I would feel it the moment I met her. I felt like saluting."

"Oh, God," said Du Pré, "don't do that."

A young man with short hair and a short beard came in the back door one step, another man behind him, very big and very black.

"Sir?" said the young bearded man.

"I think we're OK, Chad," said Vandevander, "we'll eat soon."

"That's good," boomed the black man, "I was about to slice a few chops off the lieutenant here."

"And that is Sergeant Leroy Mullins," said Vandevander. "He sings bass in the clubhouse chorus."

The four soldiers went out the back door.

"We'll wait out on the porch," said Vandevander. "Please let us know when you aren't too busy."

And they were gone.

Madelaine came back through the door. There was nothing on the ready shelf.

"Those the soldiers?" she said. "Helped a lot."

"Yeah," said Susan Klein, "they eat free, for sure."

"They want to come eat when you are not so busy," said Du Pré.

"Go get them," said Susan. "We've passed the big rush, I'm sure."

"They are on the front porch," said Du Pré.

Madelaine grinned.

"So I go and get them," she said.

The big dishwasher was drying, so it would be ten or so minutes before Du Pré could unload it.

He put on his shirt and he went out to the bar and he made himself a stiff ditch.

He looked up. Madelaine was seating the four soldiers at the round table. There were still a few plates and glasses at one side. She swept them off and she took the tub to the back.

Du Pré wandered over to the round table.

"Please join us," said Vandevander.

Du Pré sat. "Thanks," he said.

"Our pleasure," said Vandevander.

"This is a nice place," said Sergeant Mullins. He looked around very amiably.

"They have big slabs of beef here, Leroy," said Sanchez. "We can get you full up. They may have to slaughter another cow, but we'll do it."

"I could eat, all right," rumbled Mullins.

Madelaine came back with two pitchers of beer and glasses. She looked round the table. "I'll get what you want," she said, walking back toward the kitchen.

"La Salle was definitely right," said Vandevander. "Now, men, we will eat what is put before us, agreed?"

Chorus of *yessir*s.

"We will tip heavily," said Vandevander.

Chorus of *yessir*s.

Du Pré drank from his ditch.

"No offense," said Mullins, looking at Vandevander, "but if she could be persuaded to enlist, well, she has an air of natural command, sir . . ."

"None taken," said Vandevander. "We can stay home and we will just send her."

"Thank you, sir," said Mullins.

Madelaine and Jacqueline came back with huge platters holding thick slabs of prime rib, mounds of mashed potatoes with garlic and sour cream, and a set of utensils.

They set the platters down in front of the men.

"Rare, medium, rare, well done," said Madelaine, pointing to the four men, one at a time.

"How the hell she know that?" said Mullins, when Madelaine and Jacqueline walked away.

"I would be afraid to find out," said Vandevander. Du Pré laughed and so did they. Idries came in, saw them, walked over.

He sat and shortly a platter appeared, and a pitcher of soda.

Mullins looked woefully at the tiny remains of dinner on his plate. Madelaine brought another platter. Mullins brightened a lot. "If she ain't leading," said Mullins, "I ain't goin'."

Idries looked happier than he had looked.

He looked very happy indeed.

· Chapter 10 ·

PIDGEON WALKED AROUND the small white house, newly painted, and she looked at the flower beds, which were wan and weedy.

"It's going to take some work," she said.

"We've been at your place long enough," said Hoyt Poe. "We don't mind work. We always been workin', little town we come from, you worked soon as you could walk . . ."

"That we did," said Sandra.

"I got some savings," said Hoyt. "And I guess there is work out to the ranch."

Pidgeon looked at Du Pré.

"I don't know," she said.

Du Pré shrugged.

. . . Proud people, they did not want charity . . . he thought.

"Do you need household goods?" said Pidgeon.

"We got ours," said Sandra, "and they'll be along. We been sorta camping anyway since all this started, the trial and all, and then the bomb . . ."

"Bomb," said Pidgeon.

"We had this old car Hoyt's daddy give us," said Sandra, "an' while Hoyt was testifyin' there at Camp Lejuene

somebody put this bomb under the car someplace. But those
security fellas found it and took it apart 'fore it went off . . ."

"Good sweet Christ," said Pidgeon.

"I hadn't really believed there was people wantin' to kill
us 'cause of Hoyt testifyin' and sending those pictures to
headquarters, but then I believed it. Made us get rid of the old
car, as it was too easy to spot. And Hoyt finished testifyin' and
then we started livin' here and there in motels, you know, till
we come here . . ."

"It's those damned bastards from Temple," said Hoyt.

"Temple Security?" said Pidgeon.

"Yeah," said Hoyt, "they are out of Dallas you know,
operatin' in a lot of places. Private contractors. They all call
themselves Christians, you know, not Sandy and my kind,
ones think if World War Three starts Jesus will come back."

"We think he will come back," said Sandy, "but when no
one knows."

Pidgeon nodded grimly. "La Salle knows all about this, of
course," she said.

"Yes, ma'am," said Hoyt. "Those people, I don't even
want to call them soldiers, was torturing them Afghans, they
said Temple paid them to do that, they was just doin' what
they was told to do. Temple Security, not the United States
Army, they sure weren't soldiers."

Pidgeon nodded. "Well," she said, "I think you ought to
stay in the guesthouse a while longer, you know. I hadn't
thought of Temple."

"We don't want to be a bother," said Hoyt.

"Mr. Poe," said Pidgeon, "you are in danger, so is your
wife, and your daughter. Temple is a right-wing fascist army,
owned by Lloyd Cutler. One of the benefits of the current love
affair with military contractors. I know you don't want to be
a bother, but I am going to be really bothered if you move out
here. You just come back to the guesthouse for a while. We
can get this sorted out."

Hoyt and Sandra walked a little ways away, looked back, then went round behind the house.

"You know about Temple?" said Du Pré.

"The great love for private enterprise," said Pidgeon, "translated into a bunch of nutcases who gave a lot of money to politicians who then awarded contracts. Standard corruption, America has always had it, always will. What's different about these people is they are flat crazy. Right-wing loons and the worst sort of vicious, hypocritical bible bangers. They are blind fanatics and they are very dangerous, not just to the Poes, to the country. That goddamned Cutler bastard made his money in the 'oil bidness' and then he did real estate, lots of that overseas, where he has fat accounts he does not recall he has at tax time. And he does a lot of data processing for the government. Lots of it . . ."

Du Pré nodded.

"We've always had 'em," said Pidgeon. "That asshole Hoover was one. The sorry truth is most of the American people don't know what the founders were doing with the Constitution and if they did, they wouldn't like it anyway. The Bill of Rights would fail in a national referendum. The founders were concerned with the great problem of the day: could a government be created that would protect the people from the state and from each other, and not get fucked up by the very morons it was to govern."

Du Pré laughed.

"But this is no joke," said Pidgeon. "If those pigs in Temple Security are after the Poes, that is dangerous. They all have a personal relationship with Jesus, who wears jackboots and a Hitler mustache. Shit, listen to me. I got every kind of people this country has fucked over in me and I still love the place."

They laughed.

The Poes came round the house.

"We'll stay with you," said Hoyt, "if we can pay rent."

"Fine," said Pidgeon. "Two hundred a month then."

"That ain't enough," said Hoyt.

"It's fair," said Pidgeon, "prices here aren't as high as other places."

Sandra looked at her gratefully.

"Be handy to work," said Poe.

"Yes," said Pidgeon, "it would and you could start in the morning."

Poe brightened.

So did Sandra.

Little Faith Helen was tired and cranky and she needed a nap. She began to pull on her mother's hand.

"Come on, honey," said Sandra.

Pidgeon put them in the SUV and she waved at Du Pré and she drove off toward home.

Du Pré sighed, went to his cruiser, got in.

He drove up to the saloon.

There was a big yellow semitrailer parked across the road. It had a moving company's logo on the sides.

Du Pré went into the saloon.

The driver and his helper were sitting at the bar.

"They are looking for the Poes," said Susan Klein. "I never heard of them."

. . . Jesus Christ . . . thought Du Pré.

"This place is a damn long way from any place at all," said the driver.

"I will help you," said Du Pré.

The men went out to the truck.

Du Pré looked at Susan Klein, and then he turned away.

"What?" she said.

"Nothing," said Du Pré.

At his direction, the moving company people unloaded the Poes' possessions onto the street.

Du Pré signed for the couple. "I am their uncle," he said.

"Good," said the driver, "'cause we still got a long way to go." And they drove away.

There wasn't a lot. A few cardboard boxes, a chair, a child's bed with high slat sides. Du Pré got all of it into his old cruiser.

He drove out to Bart's, helped Hoyt carry the stuff into the guesthouse.

"Thanks," said Sandra. She unpacked a green glass bowl, old by the looks of it, and she put it on the sideboard.

"My great-great-granny carried that all the way from Georgiaoto, Texas," she said. "It's all I got of hers, more'n a hundred years old . . ." Hoyt stared at Sandra and his face reddened.

"Sandy," he said, "we left the bowl and this stuff with your mother. How'd your mother know to send it all here? You was told not to contact anyone, Sandy. No one at all . . ."

"I din't want Mama to worry," said Sandra. "I just sent her an email said we was all right and could she send up our stuff . . . that was all . . . wan't hardly nothin'. . ." She pouted a little.

. . . That foolish young woman . . . doesn't understand at all . . .

Du Pré walked to the main house and he went in.

"Pidgeon!" he said.

She came out of the back.

"What?" she said.

"Moving van just came to Toussaint," said Du Pré. "With all the stuff, the Poes'. Sandra wrote her mother, send it."

"Jesus Christ," said Pidgeon. She flushed, flaming angry.

She went to the telephone and she punched in some numbers she read out of an address book.

"Samantha Pidgeon," said Pidgeon, "and he damned well better talk to me." She waited for a few moments.

"The Poes blew it," she said. "Their belongings from their hometown were just delivered here."

She listened, explained, held the telephone away from her ear.

"Yeah," she said, "he told me. He's right here."

Du Pré took the telephone.

"This," said Jack La Salle, "is no good at all. It wasn't us, at least, thank God."

"*Non*," said Du Pré. "Sandra Poe, she does not believe us, so she sends word to her mother."

"I have to call Vandevander," said La Salle. "If I can't reach him, can you find him? They're training somewhere up in the mountains."

"Yah," said Du Pré.

"I'll find out what I can to help," said La Salle, "but as it's already done, just try to keep them safe."

"OK," said Du Pré.

"Shit," said La Salle.

"Shit," said Du Pré.

Pidgeon got very calm and she invited the Poes to have supper with her and Du Pré. Sandra was sulky and she seemed to feel persecuted over something very unimportant.

· **Chapter 11** ·

DU PRÉ SADDLED HIS buckskin mountain horse. The big gelding was eager to go. Walkin' John liked it up high where he looked out upon his lands and found them good.

Pidgeon came out of the house. She was dressed casually, in jeans and a worn work shirt and hat and a Glock nine-millimeter. She waved at Du Pré.

Du Pré mounted the big horse, patted the bedroll on the saddle belts, checked the saddlebags that hung below.

Du Pré rode over to Pidgeon, who was standing on her porch.

"I will find Vandevander and his men," said Du Pré.

"They have to check in tomorrow night, according to La Salle," said Pidgeon. "Worse comes to worst, I think I can manage. You know, I was rummaging through my boxes and found a Heckler and Koch submachine gun and even a dozen stun grenades. Forgot I had 'em."

Du Pré laughed.

"That was bad," said Pidgeon, "that crap with their stuff."

"Yah," said Du Pré, "it was."

"They are nice people," said Pidgeon, "but I'm not sure either of them quite gets how much danger they are in."

"*Non*," said Du Pré.

"You take care," said Pidgeon, "I hear there are bears up there . . ."

Du Pré nodded, clucked to the horse, who turned and headed for the green swing gate that went to the big pasture and the trail to the mountains.

It was late afternoon. But the days were very long now.

. . . I got five, six hours . . . thought Du Pré.

He had a pocket full of notes on heavy paper, to leave here and there. If the men were training, they might not show themselves but they might well read a note.

The horses in the pasture came over to see about Du Pré and the friend of theirs he was riding, and then they tossed their heads and ran off.

Du Pré went through the high gate and he started on the switchback trail that wound up to the long ledge cut into the mountain.

There were four Special Forces soldiers up there practicing invisibility. And Idries.

They were all very good at that, no doubt.

Du Pré saw a shadow on the ground, looked up; one of the golden eagles who nested on the cliff face was flying low above him.

Du Pré got to the ledge, looked at the trail and the stands of grass, went on.

Nothing had passed but elk and deer, a bear, and one mountain lion, young, probably male, weighed maybe seventy pounds.

Du Pré rode on, the horse picking up his pace on the flatter ground.

. . . There is only the eighteen hundred square miles of the Wolf Mountains, this is easy . . .

. . . But they will find me, not me find them . . .

Du Pré left a note on a branch near the trail, punching the end of the dead wood through the paper, and then he went on.

. . . Lots of springs, lots of places to hide . . .

• • •

By nightfall Du Pré had gotten to a small lake to the west of the mountain flank, about five or six acres of water, and deep enough so that fish could live through the winter in it. There were fat mallards nesting in the cattails by the shore and a blue heron stood at the high end of the lake, where the stream rushed in.

Du Pré hobbled the buckskin and he made a light camp, putting his bedroll and henskin under a spruce tree that had branches low to the ground.

The chill started, rolling down from the peaks, and Du Pré made a small fire in a small hole, and he sat near it, feeling the heat rise.

He chewed jerky, deer meat jerky, the real stuff, sundried, rubbed with garlic and salt. It broke apart in the mouth and bloomed with flavor.

He had whiskey from a half-gallon plastic jug, rolled a smoke, lit it.

He heard movement.

Du Pré looked over at where the sound had come from.

Benetsee appeared suddenly, the little light shone on his face, a glow from the fire.

"Ah," said the old man, "so you have come here to bring me a smoke and some whiskey."

"No whiskey," said Du Pré. "Your doctor said no more."

"I don't got a doctor," said Benetsee, "they are ver' dangerous people. They know a little but they don't know anything of any use . . ."

Du Pré laughed.

"I am looking for the soldiers," he said.

Benetsee nodded.

"They will come," he said. "Bad thing, those young people, little girl."

Du Pré had long since given up trying to figure out how Benetsee knew what he knew.

He just did.

But since it was Du Pré looking for the soldiers, God alone knew what the old bastard would do to have his little jokes.

"You don't do nothing to those soldiers," said Du Pré.

"Whiskey," said Benetsee, "or I turn you into a worm, step on you."

Du Pré handed the old man the bottle.

Gluggal glurg gluggal glurg.

"Christ," said Du Pré, "you sound like a bad drain."

"You are young and healthy," said Benetsee. "More of this I drink you don't get. I am helping you, long life."

"Christ," said Du Pré.

Gluggal glurg gluggal glurg.

"You old bastard," said Du Pré.

They heard a human voice then.

"FUCK!" it said.

A hoglike sound, too, a snuffling, then the sound of branches being torn off a tree.

"Oh, for Chrissakes," said Du Pré.

"Shit! SHIT!" said the voice.

Benetsee smiled.

"I think," he said, "that is someone up a tree bear wants to climb into, also."

"SHIT!" said the voice again. "I will shoot you, you bastard."

Benetsee got up in one smooth motion and he disappeared into the dark.

The sounds changed, now something very heavy was moving off.

"You were a lot of goddamned help," said the voice.

"Well," said the deep rich basso of Sergeant Mullins, "he seemed to want to talk to the commander and not a simple sergeant. Besides, we were told we couldn't shoot any animals."

"Goddamn it, Sergeant," said Colonel Vandevander, "that fucking bear was bigger'n you are."

"Yes, sir," said Mullins. "I thought perhaps I would let rank deal with it, sir."

Du Pré walked toward the voices.

"Who goes there," said Mullins.

"Du Pré," said Du Pré.

"Du Pré," said Vandevander, "I would really appreciate it if you sort of forgot all this."

"*Non*," said Du Pré.

"There go my general's stars then," said Vandevander.

"No one will believe it anyway," said Sergeant Mullins, "how the baddest of the bad, who are so tough we got muscles in our shit, were run up trees by a bear."

"That fucking thing was *huge*," said Vandevander.

"Medium," said Du Pré.

"That was a *medium* bear? It is *dangerous* up here." Vandevander landed on the ground. Mullins came down, too, a little more heavily.

There were shouts coming from farther up the mountain.

"Does that animal eat people or just run them up trees?" said Vandevander.

"So far," said Du Pré, "so good."

More shouts.

"They have bears in Kazakhstan," said Mullins. "I read that."

Then there was a ripping crashing sound of trees breaking and then silence.

"What kind of bear was that?" said Vandevander.

"A grizzly," said Du Pré, "but he is gone now."

"They got grizzlies in Kazakhstan?" said Vandevander.

"Oh, no," said Mullins, "the Kazakh bears ran them all over here to America . . . on account them grizzlies was such wussies. Right across that Bering Land Bridge. Used to connect A-Laska to Siberia but it done got drownded by global warming."

"Mullins," said Vandevander, "fuck you . . ."

· Chapter 12 ·

"THIS WHOLE BUSINESS is crap on crap," said La Salle over the satellite phone. "These morons are destroying our reputation in the world. And for nothing. You never get anything using torture. If you use it, you've lost."

"Yah," said Du Pré.

"They're a bunch of sick perverts," said La Salle. "Ah, why am I even explaining this to you?"

"I don't know," said Du Pré.

"Word's come down: Vandevander and the others have to get back to their training," said La Salle. "I'm sorry but there it is."

"OK," said Du Pré.

"I know there will be a reckoning with these bastards," said La Salle, "I just wish it would come on."

"Yah," said Du Pré.

"Let me speak to Vandevander," said La Salle.

Du Pré handed the satellite phone back to the colonel. Idries had materialized out of nowhere and he was trying very hard to keep a straight face and not entirely succeeding.

Du Pré walked away from Vandevander so he couldn't hear any of the conversation.

Mullins was lying down, head on a log. He looked comfortable. He couldn't be, but he looked like he was.

"Huge bears," said Idries, "their tracks are like . . . washtubs."

"That's what I heard," said Mullins.

"Du Pré," said Lieutenant Chasen, "what happened with that damn bear? It found all of us, ran us all up trees, and I swear when it walked away it was *laughing.*"

"Benetsee," said Du Pré.

"And what is a Bennett-see?" said Chasen.

"He is a medicine person," said Du Pré.

"Oh," said Chasen. "Does he change himself into bears and shit?"

"I don't know," said Du Pré. "I have never actually seen him do it."

"Yeah, they do," said Mullins. "I read about that."

"It happens," said Sanchez. "Part of my family lives in the high mountains in Mexico, with the Yaquis and Huichols and I heard the stories."

"The only one he didn't bother was Idries," said Chasen. "You got some sort of secret?"

Idries grinned.

"Yes," he said, "but it is so secret I can't tell you."

Vandevander came over.

"We have to go on with the exercise tomorrow night," he said.

"Practice climbing trees ahead of bears?" said Du Pré.

"Shit," said Vandevander.

An owl hooted.

The soldiers were all on the ground with pistols out in a few seconds.

"It is Benetsee," said Du Pré.

The soldiers relaxed.

"Owl sounds are easy for humans to mimic," said Chasen, "so we assume that is what we are hearing."

"Will he come in?" said Vandevander. "I'd like to meet him."

"I don't know," said Du Pré.

"So whaddaya want us ta do in the meantime?" said Sanchez. "Go guard the Poes or go back to climbing trees in the woods here, get good at it. Idries says there are huge bears in Kazakhstan."

"Idries," said Vandevander, "is full of shit."

"That," said Idries, "is a rotten way to talk about an ally."

"You didn't have to climb a tree," said Vandevander.

"I spoke briefly with your friend, Benetsee," said Idries to Du Pré, "to tell him my grandfather is coming. Great-grandfather, actually. He laughed and said the two of them would find ways to make your life hell."

"We're ready," said Mullins. He had a huge pack on his back and a strange long rifle in his hand.

The men had disappeared by the time Du Pré broke camp. The buckskin, Walkin' John, could find his way back easily enough and Du Pré gave the horse his head. The big horse whuffled a few times and then he began to move down the trail, sure and quick on his feet.

Du Pré rode with his head down and his hat tipped forward. Walkin' John was a scamp and he would try to run Du Pré into a branch if he could.

Du Pré dozed, awakening when he felt the soft touch of pine needles on his hat. Walkin' John was having trouble finding the right branch to scrape Du Pré off with.

It took about as much time to go down as it did to come up, and it was getting light when Du Pré came through the last gate. He put Walkin' John in a stall in the big barn and he went to the little cabin Bart had given him.

"You need a place to hide out from Madelaine," Bart had said.

The cabin was musty. Du Pré opened all the windows and he took a shower and he got into bed, after peeling the sheets and blankets back to check for spiders.

No spiders.

He fell asleep.

Du Pré woke up to knocking.

Pidgeon was standing at the door. Du Pré pulled on his pants and a shirt.

"Those guys are good," said Pidgeon. "I was in the shadow, watching for people, and I was staying damn still and some voice sounded like it came out of a well said, 'Go to sleep, missy, we got it.' Then the guy came out of *his* shadow. He was damn near as big as my house."

"You met Mullins," said Du Pré.

"Yes," said Pidgeon, "and when it got light, the others, as well. They came in for breakfast. And then they said that they had to go back up. They have their orders."

Du Pré yawned.

"So," said Pidgeon, "I have breakfast stuff left over and the Poes are up at the house. That is a darling little girl . . ." and Pidgeon looked wistful.

"OK," said Du Pré.

"The guys told me about a bear last night," said Pidgeon.

"Benetsee and his games," said Du Pré.

"I thought so," said Pidgeon and left.

"I'll be up," said Du Pré. He dressed and pulled on his boots, stuck his Glock in the holster at the small of his back. He punched his hat a few times but without much effect.

He walked up to the house.

Pidgeon was looking both angry and worried.

"Temple got to the Poe stuff. Hoyt just gave me this. Found it when he unpacked the last box this morning." She held out a small gray cylinder a half inch in diameter and four inches long.

"It's an incendiary," said Pidgeon. "Those bastards would burn these good people alive."

Du Pré nodded.

"Can Benetsee help?" said Pidgeon.

"I don't know," said Du Pré. "He is strange, you know."

"Bart is supposed to be back tonight," said Pidgeon.

"I stay here," said Du Pré.

"Good," said Pidgeon. "And now I am going to go and call Foote."

Charles Foote, Bart's lawyer. In his forties, elegant, observant.

A very well-educated cobra.

"And after Foote," said Pidgeon, "I'm calling Harvey."

Harvey Wallace, Pidgeon's old boss at the FBI.

"Say hi for me," said Du Pré.

"You believe this shit?" said Pidgeon.

"Yah," said Du Pré.

He heard a horse running and a child's shriek of fear and joy.

They went out to the porch.

Pallas was on Stewball and Faith Helen was sitting in front of her, holding on to the saddle horn.

They were both laughing.

They both waved as they went past.

Hoyt and Sandra looked at their daughter and they both glowed with pride.

· Chapter 13 ·

"I WILL GO and get them," said Pidgeon. "You haven't slept in a while. Idries needs to go too; he says he must honor his great-grandfather. God, that old bastard must be over a hundred."

"No," said Idries, "we marry early, if we have the money."

"You're married?" said Pidgeon.

Idries saddened, his face one of wintry grief. "My wife was killed, along with our two children, in a plane crash two years ago," he said. "They were flying to Almaty to see her parents. Our airlines aren't as safe as they should be."

"Oh, God," said Pidgeon, "I am so sorry. Please forgive me."

Idries nodded. "You could not know," he said.

There was a long silence.

The telephone chirred. Pidgeon went to answer. Her low voice made a few terse replies. She came back.

"That was Foote," she said. "He said things may be even worse than we thought. Temple Security was a very small outfit until 9/11, and then they truly prospered. You don't work for them unless you are a foaming fascist. And they have Bible study groups, compulsory. Foote said it is a simple matter to deal with people who are rational, however crooked. The Temple bunch, however, is insane, the entire two thousand of them, all trained soldiers and all religious fanatics who have frequent conversations with Jesus . . ."

"Ah," said Idries, "people of my faith have had encounters with those people over the centuries . . ." And he looked very sad.

"What about the Poes?" said Du Pré.

"Vandevander will see to them," said Idries, "until there is another arrangement. We discussed it and concluded that although he was ordered to resume training, *when* he does that was left . . . open."

Du Pré laughed.

"I will be happy to stay here, too, can use the rest," said Du Pré. "I am old."

"Uh-huh," said Pidgeon. She turned to Idries. "Tell me about your great-grandfather."

"Mukhtar Khan is an eagle hunter," said Idries. "He trains them to hunt from his arm."

"Kazakhs use eagles as falcons?" said Pidgeon. "Jesus, those birds are huge . . ."

"Yes," said Idries, "Mukhtar Khan hunted wolves with them."

Du Pré nodded.

Idries was smiling. "I will enjoy his meeting with Benetsee," he said.

They walked out to one of the big SUVs the ranch kept. Pidgeon got in the driver's door, Idries the passenger's.

"Keep an eye on those kids," said Pidgeon.

Du Pré nodded. He looked over toward the guesthouse.

Sandra and little Faith Helen were digging in a flower bed. The little girl picked up something that glittered. Du Pré laughed.

"I buried a few treasures," said Pidgeon. "Nothing better for a little girl than finding a tiara and washing the mud off the rhinestones." She started the engine; it caught and purred. "See ya," said Pidgeon.

She drove the SUV down toward the county road.

Du Pré wandered over to the guesthouse.

Hoyt Poe came out, dressed in jeans and a faded shirt and old scuffed boots. "Hat got lost in the shuffle," he said. "It was just an old straw one but it kept the sun off."

. . . He needs to work . . . Du Pré thought.

"We got stuff for you, in the barn," said Du Pré.

"Great," said Hoyt.

They walked past the main house to the big barn. It was cool and dark and smelled of hay and horse piss.

Du Pré pulled a straw hat off a peg in the tack room.

"If this fits," he said, "you can have it. Somebody left it here, hung there for years . . ."

Hoyt tried it. It was a little large. "I'll just stuff the band a little," he said. "It's fine."

"You work horses?" said Du Pré.

"Yes, sir," said Hoyt.

"Saddles are there," said Du Pré, pointing, "blankets, headstalls, catch ropes. There are four geldings need to be ridden . . ."

Hoyt nodded. "You favor one sort of trainin' over another?" he said, looking earnestly at Du Pré.

Du Pré shrugged.

Hoyt looked out at the horses in the pasture.

"Mister Du Pré," he said, "I feel you are testin' me. Well, all right. I don't favor bein' hard on stock. I like horses, try to understand them, they's all different and they's different day to day."

Du Pré laughed. "OK," he said, "I just wanted to know if you worked horses . . ."

"And didn't beat the shit out of 'em 'cause I didn't know how to work horses," said Hoyt, smiling.

"You work on a ranch?" said Du Pré.

"Well, I did, for a time," said Hoyt. "Where I come from there was two ranches owned by rich folks and a bunch of people worked for them or at the chicken plant, cuttin' up chickens. 'Bout all there was there, 'less you was a good mechanic, or maybe you played good football, get a scholarship. You seen them towns. Good people, poor people, less'n a thousand folks, most of them born right there. One big church and maybe six smaller ones. Place big northern money comes to, build a chicken plant or a place makes frozen tacos. People need work, they ain't gonna get them a union, get more money . . ."

Du Pré nodded.

"So I started thinkin' about joinin' up," said Hoyt, "and after my pa was killed it was all there was to do. Sandy agreed with me. I got good eyesight, real good, so I did all the basic stuff, then went to sniper school, then to demolition school, did pretty well. Then Afghanistan. I been blown up three times and shot twice. One of them blown-up times I was the only one in the Humvee wasn't mangled. Everybody else lost something, arm, leg, both, all, an eye, their life . . ."

Du Pré nodded. He looked at the young man.

"So after I got patched up they put me on prison duty, temporary, and that was where I seen all that stuff, the bastards making pictures of it all, keepsakes, you might say . . ."

Du Pré nodded.

"I didn't think it was right, Mister Du Pré," said Hoyt. "It was just what we call where I come from blood mean. So I went up the chain of command. Got told to shut up, but I would not, and here I am . . ."

"You did the right thing," said Du Pré.

"Maybe for me," said Hoyt. "But Sandy and Faith Helen, maybe not. Oh, Sandy has said I did the right thing and she's proud of me, but, hell, I done put them in danger and a man isn't supposed to do that . . ."

"They will be all right," said Du Pré. "If there were not people like you, we would all be in danger."

Hoyt nodded, but his eyes were a little wet.

"I'm sorry," he said, wiping them.

. . . Poor guy, takes the oath and thinks everybody believes it just like he did . . .

"I don't have gloves with me," said Hoyt, "we didn't have any time . . ."

"Come on," said Du Pré.

They walked out to his old cruiser. He opened the trunk. He had several pairs of gloves, new, in a plastic bag. The .50-caliber rifle he had bought years before and fired once was in there, too, in its case.

Hoyt looked at the case.

Du Pré flipped the latches. He opened the lid.

The huge rifle sat in green foam, black, dull finished, the spare magazines loaded with cartridges.

"Goddamn," said Hoyt, "that's that civilian one supposed to be damned good, all custom bedded . . ."

Du Pré handed the rifle to Hoyt.

Hoyt looked at it, took the caps off the telescopic sight. "Use this for coyotes?" said Hoyt.

"Yah," said Du Pré. "Once."

The coyote had been a good mile away, out of range for any rifle but the .50-caliber.

Du Pré had put his jacket on the roof of his cruiser, used a bag of salt for a mount, put the crosshairs on the coyote, counted the steps for the yardage, and had squeezed the trigger. The rifle kicked like hell. Du Pré had pulled his eye away from the telescopic sight, so he saw the coyote die.

It had blown up, exploded, disintegrated. Du Pré had put the big rifle back in the case and he hadn't taken it out again, until now.

He looked up at the big pasture, saw Pallas riding hell-for-leather down the mountain.

She opened the gate and Stewball stepped through, dancing a little. He liked to run.

She and Stewball got up to speed. Pallas rode like she was another piece of the horse.

Du Pré went out to the round corral, where Hoyt was trying to dap a loop over one or another horse's head. The horses knew enough to dodge the rope.

Hoyt stopped when he saw Pallas.

"She can ride some," he said.

Du Pré pointed back toward the mountain.

Berkut shot out of the forest and he leaped over the barbed-wire fence, clearing it handily.

The dog raced after Pallas and Stewball.

They all got to where Du Pré was looking through the fence at about the same time. Pallas laughed as she had not in a long time.

She got down.

Du Pré looked at his granddaughter and then at Hoyt.

"You can sure ride," the young man said.

Pallas looked back at him.

She nodded.

"Where is your wife and little girl?"

"At the guesthouse I guess you'd call it," said Hoyt.

"I will take your daughter for a ride," said Pallas, getting back on Stewball, who ambled off. A few minutes later they came back, and little Faith Helen was holding on to the saddle horn in front of Pallas. She was laughing and looking very proud. Pallas rode off with her, laughing.

. . . She is laughing and not just to make us feel better . . . thought Du Pré.

He saw something out of the corner of his eye, and when he turned it was Madelaine's little station wagon, dark green with tinted windows.

She parked and walked over to Du Pré.

"She is better, I think," said Du Pré, "that Skull Springs water maybe."

Madelaine looked at him.

"Du Pré," she said, "do you really think, the water?"

Du Pré looked at her.

Madelaine was shielding her eyes and staring at the eagles soaring.

· Chapter 14 ·

DU PRÉ SAT IN the saloon, sipping his ditch and watching the news. It was all bad. It was usually all bad. There were a dozen or so people in the place, eating burgers or just drinking. A couple of young cowboys were playing pool and joshing each other. They would have a fistfight in half an hour or so, but they would go out in back, it was only good manners.

"They will be here soon," said Madelaine. "And how is Hoyt Poe?"

"Good with horses," said Du Pré.

"Those poor kids," said Madelaine. "Ever' day I see those bastards have done something else, Washington, worst people I ever heard of . . ."

Du Pré nodded.

He went out of the front door then, stood on the long porch, rolled a smoke. The summer night air was flowing down from the mountains, though there was still plenty of light.

A big dark SUV came down the western road. Du Pré waited. It pulled up and stopped.

The doors opened and Bart and Pidgeon got out, and then Idries, and then Booger Tom, who waited, grinning, by the door.

Mukhtar Khan jumped down, nimbly. He wore a tunic, a wide leather belt, baggy trousers, high boots, and a soft round hat. He looked up at the front of the saloon.

Idries said something to him. Mukhtar Khan replied. Then a voice spoke in a language that Du Pré had never heard; it had what he thought might be Shoshone words in it, but might not.

Benetsee, somewhere near, but not in sight.

Mukhtar Khan laughed, he turned to look at Idries, and then he trotted around the side of the saloon.

Bart shook his head.

"What was that about?" he said.

"Two very, very old men having their little joke," said Idries.

Bart nodded.

"It is said that Mukhtar can change into other creatures," said Idries, "but of course that is impossible."

Du Pré nodded.

"Well," said Pidgeon, "why don't we get something to eat and keep an eye peeled for mangy old critters that speak in tongues?"

They all laughed.

"He isn't wearing his bandoliers," said Idries. "I have never seen him without them."

They went in and sat at the big round table.

Madelaine came over. She didn't bother with the menus, or with asking anyone what they might want.

She went off toward the kitchen, and soon she was back with drinks.

Du Pré sighed and he rolled a smoke. He took a long swallow of his ditch.

"They should get on well," said Idries.

"Better'n that," said Booger Tom. "Hell, they even look alike."

The old cowboy grinned. His washed-out blue eyes twinkled.

"Heard you had trouble with a bear," he said, looking at Idries.

"Ah, not me," said Idries, "the four Americans were . . . troubled. They have orders not to shoot anything, so they all had to climb trees . . ."

"That big old bastard's usually up the Necklace Lakes now," said Booger Tom, "odd he'd be down any lower."

"Well," said Idries, "he was."

"How was the flight?" said Pidgeon.

"If you like flyin' it was fine," said Booger Tom. "Very luxurious airplane. I gather one of them planes costs about as much as a small country."

Bart nodded.

"On the other hand," said Booger Tom, "when you kin fly halfway around the damn world with one fill-up stop out and one stop comin' back, it is mighty convenient."

The food came and they ate.

"How's Hoyt doing?" said Bart, "and the little girl and . . . Sandra?"

"Good," said Du Pré. "He is a good hand with horses."

"Where's he from?" said Booger Tom.

"Texas," said Du Pré.

"Oh," said Booger Tom, his face souring.

"Listen, you old son of a bitch," said Pidgeon, "you are not going to give that kid crap because he is a Texan."

"But . . ." said Booger Tom, "he's a *Texan*."

Pidgeon glared at him.

"All right," he said.

They finished eating and they left and Du Pré went to the bar, where Madelaine sat, rubbing lotion on her hands.

"You see the old guy from Kazakhstan?" said Madelaine.

"Yes," said Du Pré.

"You see who he looks like?" said Madelaine.

"Like Benetsee," said Du Pré.

She nodded.

"They speak the same language," said Madelaine. "Old language."

Du Pré nodded.

"Du Pré," said Madelaine, "you grew up here, you got that scholarship, went to college, the army, then you came back here. Why you do that?"

Du Pré laughed. "It is home," he said.

Madelaine nodded.

"But," she said, "you could have lived someplace else, come back here to visit."

Du Pré rolled a cigarette, lit it, passed it to her. She took her one puff.

"I lived other places," said Du Pré. "I could have done other work. But I was always lonely other places. Here there is old blood, my people are part of this dust here, this grass, this water . . ."

Madelaine nodded.

"Why you ask me that now?" said Du Pré.

"You like old things," said Madelaine, "old stories, old songs; you like the stories about the Red Ocher People coming down here fifty thousand years ago, you like them a lot . . ."

Du Pré laughed. "I might go there, Kazakhstan," he said, "but I come back."

Madelaine looked at him. "OK," she said.

"I do want to know that story," said Du Pré, "one tells about Benetsee and Mukhtar Khan."

"I know," said Madelaine.

"That is all," said Du Pré.

"OK," said Madelaine.

"You want to come too," said Du Pré.

Madelaine nodded.

Du Pré reached out and he patted Madelaine's hand. It was still a little wet with lotion.

"Things change," said Madelaine, "people die. This place is dying, there are people leaving, not many, but there are not many here. Nothing for the young people."

Du Pré nodded.

"What you do when Benetsee dies?" said Madelaine.

Du Pré nodded, looked somber.

"I got this feeling," said Madelaine, "when Mukhtar Khan comes and he and Benetsee talk, it is the end of something."

Du Pré looked at her.

She rubbed her hands.

"You are sad," said Du Pré.

Madelaine nodded. "You remember when . . . it was that old man, Canada, Mipsi?"

Du Pré nodded. . . . Another medicine person . . . "What does he have to do with this?" said Du Pré.

"He said once that we had people far, far away, over the ocean and desert and mountains. That they lived in the mountains and they rode horses and they carried eagles on their wrists to hunt with and they spoke our language."

Du Pré nodded.

"Mipsi said if any of us ever met any of them, then the world would end . . ." said Madelaine.

Du Pré nodded. "If I go there," he said, "you come too."

"Pallas is going there," said Madelaine, "she falls in love with Idries. They neither one know it yet but Pallas is happier now because of Idries. I think he is a good man, but it is so very far away."

"Nothing is very far away now," said Du Pré. "It is one of the big problems people have."

· Chapter 15 ·

"NASTY," SAID HARVEY Wallace. He looked again at the incendiary device. "But I wonder why it failed."

Du Pré looked at him. "Somehow Temple people got to the stuff."

"I also wonder," said Harvey, "why I keep finding you in the mix. You live in the ass end of nowhere at all and you despise the twenty-first century. Yet now you have another crop of high-tech wingnuts. I ought to put you in my budgetary requests. Couple million for Du Pré, he attracts armed loons."

Two technicians were going through everything the Poes owned. Sandra and little Faith Helen were sitting on the porch outside.

"Didn't like the last century much either," said Du Pré.

Harvey nodded at the back door.

They went outside. The lilacs had just lost their blooms but the scent was still thick.

"Thing about bureaucrats," said Harvey, "is they are expert at covering their asses. Somebody fairly high up carefully deleted an email message. We have a few suspects, all of whom are indignant we could think such a thing of them. My money is on some careless talk, a joke about security, a sneer about the password."

One of the technicians came out. "Something you'd better look at," he said.

Harvey and Du Pré went inside.

The technician pointed to the computer screen.

More emails.

All to Louella Pender, in Jouvain, Texas.

Hi Mom how are you? Love, Sandy

"This woman!" said Harvey. "This is just exactly how Temple found them and she still doesn't get it."

Du Pré nodded.

"You still don't have one of these," said Harvey. It was not a question.

"*Non*," said Du Pré.

"I'll send you one," said Harvey.

"Fine," said Du Pré. "Me, I go to the dump when I need to."

They walked out to the front porch.

Harvey looked at Sandra, who looked away.

"Mrs. Poe," said Harvey, "I think you know why I'm standing here and looking pissed off. You sent emails to your mother, they were easy to intercept, and so now the people who can do that know exactly where you are."

"I couldn't let Mama worry," said Sandra.

"But you were told you were in grave danger and if you won't act like you have some good sense," said Harvey, "it may get you all killed."

Sandra stuck her thumbnail in her teeth and she nodded. Her eyes were filled with tears.

"I'm sorry," she said. "I didn't really think it would hurt nothin'."

Little Faith Helen watched her mother's face, concerned.

"The military cut you loose," said Harvey, "and we can't protect you, the FBI doesn't do that. The case was military, so you can't be protected by the Marshals Service, either. You're down to the friends you have here. You could put them in danger, too, and you may have already."

Sandra flared up, angry. "We cain't live like this!" she yelled. "Hoyt did the right thing but we cain't live like this . . ."

The technicians came out of the house; one of them shook his head.

All four men walked back toward the main ranch house.

Harvey jangled change in his pocket as they went.

"That poor, foolish girl," he said. "She simply does not apprehend how dangerous what she did was. If they are moved, she'll just do it again . . ."

Du Pré nodded.

Pidgeon came out of the house. She was wearing a crimson silk blouse and lots of silver-and-turquoise jewelry.

"Jesus," said Harvey, looking at her, "what happened to the blue pinstripe suits?"

"I don't have to not upset you guys anymore," said Pidgeon. "You know how terrified guys are all the time. Worried that everyone they meet has a longer dick or a better mind. Or worse, a better mind without any dick at all."

"Don't," said Harvey, "start in on us guys again. It's not fair."

"So whatcha find?" said Pidgeon.

"No more devices, but Sandra's still emailing her mother," said Harvey.

"Christ," said Pidgeon. "Ah, they didn't have any real cover here anyway. But it won't help to move them somewhere else, they'll just blow it there. Foote can send security people, good ones, but if the Poes won't cooperate, that won't help much. And they won't. At least, she won't."

"I think you're right," said Harvey.

Pidgeon nodded. She looked up at the sky. There were high lines of thin clouds. A storm was coming in from the west.

"You could talk to her," said Harvey.

"I did," said Pidgeon. "They wanted to live in town, which was too exposed. Then their stuff shows up, sent by ordinary moving van. That was the stuff that the Poes left with her mom and Sandy was the one who had it sent here. Nobody can make that young woman understand what she doesn't want to."

Du Pré laughed, but there was no humor in it.

"She might as well be working to get Hoyt killed," said Harvey. "He's the one they want dead, but they'll kill her, too, if it suits their purposes."

"Harvey," said Pidgeon, "are you telling me all you know? About Temple Security?"

Harvey looked off in the distance.

"You son of a bitch," said Pidgeon.

"Ongoing investigation," said Harvey.

"Uh-huh," said Pidgeon.

"You know how it is," said Harvey.

"Yeah," said Pidgeon. "How it is, is this: Hoyt is a nice guy but naive, and the military wishes he would just evaporate. They would like everyone to forget all about Temple Security and what went on in that prison. They bank on our national amnesia."

Harvey nodded. "But the army is trying to cut ties with Temple, as well, and Temple is unhappy about that, to say the least."

"Nothing more you can tell us about that firestarter?" said Pidgeon.

"No," said Harvey. "Iranian, millions of them around probably. The device is simple, cheap, and reasonably safe to them as carries."

Pidgeon nodded. "Sounds like Temple," she said.

"You know most of it already," said Harvey.

"I know they recruit Bible-thumping Nazis," said Pidgeon.

"Who think Jesus will return if they can just start World War Three," said Harvey.

Pidgeon shook her head. "Harvey," she said, "you really piss me off."

Harvey nodded.

"Nice game," said Pidgeon. "This is really about your Temple Security investigation, not the Poes' safety. The Poes are trusting and they're here and they make good bait, right? It's a perfect setup—so that makes it all right, right?"

Harvey didn't say anything.

"Land of the free, home of the brave," said Pidgeon.

"Take care," said Harvey, and he walked away.

Pidgeon looked at Du Pré.

"Wonderful world, huh?" she said.

Du Pré nodded.

· Chapter 16 ·

"ARE THOSE TWO old bastards going to be all right?" said Bart.

He was standing beside the Toussaint Saloon, looking up at the high mountains.

"Yah," said Du Pré.

"Fine state of things," said Bart. "I fly the whole goddamned way to fucking Kazakhstan, pick up Mukhtar Khan, and fly him back here and I am about to give him a feast and he has a few words with Benetsee and that's that. I hope he doesn't overstay his visa."

"If he does," said Du Pré, "what they going to do about it?"

"Du Pré," said Bart, "come over here. See if you see anything that isn't quite right."

Du Pré looked up at the mountains.

They had white snowcaps still, the day was clear, the air free of dust, and the dark flanks covered with spruce and fir and pine were a little hazy from the dew cooking off.

An eagle soared over a high pocket valley. "Maybe the other one is hunting, farther off?" said Du Pré.

"They hunt together," said Bart. "They are golden eagles."

"Yah," said Du Pré.

Madelaine came out of the back door of the saloon, saw them, and walked over.

"Those old bastards caught one of the eagles," said Bart, "I know they did. Catching an eagle is *illegal!*"

"What they going to do about that?" said Du Pré.

"Christ," said Bart, "I vouched for Mukhtar Khan."

"Benetsee, him," said Madelaine, "they pretty much do what they want, you know. They are so old they don't much care for other opinions."

Bart looked at Du Pré.

"Don't you have to get an eagle when it is young?" he said. "Take it out of the nest and train it?"

"I don't know," said Du Pré, "the eagle hunters here used to catch eagles and kill them for the feathers and bones . . ."

"They wouldn't kill it, would they?" said Bart. "That would be really illegal."

Madelaine laughed.

"What you want?" she said. "Go and get them? You have horses."

"They all hate me," said Bart. "All my horses want me dead."

"You want Du Pré to go?" said Madelaine.

Bart looked at Du Pré.

"Oh, for God's sakes," said Du Pré, "they will come down when they want to. I am not chasing them all over the Wolf Mountains. Those old bastards will make a lot of trouble for me."

"Booger Tom can do it," said Bart.

"Then you have all three of them up there," said Du Pré. "Then I really will not go."

Madelaine laughed.

"Du Pré wants to go anyway," she said, looking at Bart.

She kissed Du Pré on the cheek.

"Tell Benetsee," she said, "I have a bath ready for him."

"Sure," said Du Pré, "I carry hate mail. Why don't you write it down?"

"I'd appreciate it," said Bart. He smiled at Du Pré.

"He wants to go," said Madelaine, "he is just fucking with you."

"He would never do that," said Bart.

Du Pré walked to his cruiser, got in.

"I bring the food out for you," said Madelaine. "I am done here. You will take Walkin' John?"

"Yah," said Du Pré. "Maybe a packhorse, maybe I leave some food for the soldiers."

"They are eating out of those plastic bags," said Madelaine.

"Yah," said Du Pré, "I will look for them and if I find them, it is because they don't mind if I do."

Du Pré drove out to Bart's. He parked the cruiser by the barn and he got out and he looked up at the mountains.

"Mister Du Pré," said Hoyt, "glad you came. There's a couple horses missing. I didn't notice it right off."

Du Pré nodded.

"Some tack, too," said Hoyt.

Du Pré nodded.

"There people here at the ranch I don't know about?" said Hoyt.

"There were," said Du Pré. "I know who they are."

"So it's all right. Missus Fascelli is gone and I didn't know who to tell. Booger Tom just snorted when I told him and I guessed he didn't want to talk about it."

Du Pré nodded.

"He's pissed off they didn't ask him to come along," said Du Pré.

"Oh," said Hoyt. "Look, I'm awful sorry about Sandy and all. She's a willful girl."

Du Pré looked at him.

"She always was," said Hoyt. "Family is too. Willful people."

"It is dangerous," said Du Pré. "She doesn't seem to believe there are people out there who want to kill you."

"I have trouble believing it myself," said Hoyt. "I know they do but it don't make no sense, Mister Du Pré."

"They know that you are here now," said Du Pré, "but it is not so easy a place to get to."

"We gonna have to live the rest of our lives like this?" said Hoyt. "Raise Faith Helen to be scared all the time?"

"I don't know," said Du Pré. "Look, catch Walkin' John and that old brown packhorse, Cooter. Bring them in, I will pack up."

"Sure," said Hoyt. He went off and shortly he headed up to the pasture on a four-wheel ATV.

. . . Ver' noisy horse . . . don't have to catch it first though . . . Du Pré thought.

Du Pré went into the barn and he got down a pack frame and his saddle and bags, a bedroll, a cook kit, a linen water bag.

He piled the things on a long bench on the wall next to the big sliding doors.

Madelaine's little station wagon pulled up and she got out.

She walked into the barn.

"Pain in the ass," she said.

Du Pré nodded.

"You think they have an eagle?" said Madelaine.

Du Pré nodded.

"Well," said Madelaine, "I brought you steaks and jerky and dried fruit, whiskey, chocolate, and all the usual stuff."

"I maybe kill them and skin them," said Du Pré.

"No," said Madelaine, "you would miss Benetsee."

Du Pré nodded.

Burrupp. The ATV drove close to the barn.

Hoyt soon came in, leading Walkin' John and the packhorse.

Du Pré saddled Walkin' John while Madelaine packed the plastic panniers that fitted in the pack frame.

She had set the frame on a narrow crossboard, so she could balance the load. She finished, shut the lids, pulled first one and then the other out.

Madelaine came to Du Pré and they kissed.

"You remember," she said.

Du Pré looked at her.

"They are hunting with an eagle," said Madelaine. "I know you, you will want to go where people do that."

"They do it here," said Du Pré.

"You just remember," said Madelaine, "I go too."

Du Pré laughed.

"Anything else?" said Hoyt.

Du Pré shook his head.

"Hoyt?" said Sandra from the doorway. "Hoyt, I tol' you I needed some help." She had little Faith Helen with her. The big-eyed child held her mother's hand.

"I had work to do," said Hoyt.

"I need to go somewhere I can go shopping," said Sandra. "I got to get some things. There has be a Walmart round here someplace . . ."

"In a minute, honey," said Hoyt.

"And what'll we do about a car?" said Sandra.

Du Pré led Walkin' John out, and Hoyt brought the packhorse.

Du Pré swung up.

"Thanks," he said to Hoyt.

"Hoyt," said Sandra, "we got to get a car."

· Chapter 17 ·

DU PRÉ RODE UP the trail, looking for sign that the missing horses had passed by.

There wasn't any, but then there were many trails and Benetsee knew all of them. Knew more of them than Du Pré did. Or ever would.

He found a place where a man had crossed the trail, then tried to blur his footprints.

. . . If I see them, I tell them they need to sweep along and not across . . . Du Pré thought. . . . probably have to rewrite the whole manual then. . . . when I am in Germany waiting for the Russians to come, which they were not going to do, I look out across the plain and see one of our tanks. It is moving until its right tread comes off . . .

. . . Now our soldiers are in the Mideast, little bunches of them, fighting like Indians fought . . .

Du Pré looked up at the ridgetop. The lodgepole pines grew to perhaps fifty feet, thin and strong. But on the top there were no trees, there was too much wind and too little soil for the trees to root at all.

Benetsee and Mukhtar Khan appeared suddenly, the two old men moving very quickly.

Mukhtar had an eagle on his right arm. The huge bird was hooded and Mukhtar now had bandoliers of cartridges crossing his chest, and a bolt-action rifle.

Benetsee had a gallon jug of screw-top wine. He waved gaily at Du Pré and he gestured toward a meadow a half mile away, a place with good water and grass.

Du Pré nodded.

. . . I see them because they want to see me . . .

He went on. In ten minutes he was riding up the last steep bit of the trail and then the meadow opened up before him, an old lake bed filled now with soil and peat, grass three feet tall rooted in the damp earth.

The campsite was at the far side, a flat place set in the mountain, out of the wind and near a small clear spring that trickled down from a band of yellow rock, filling a small pool at the base. There was a wooden platform for a big wall tent, a small cast-iron woodstove wrapped in a sheet of heavy black plastic, and a pole corral big enough to put three or four horses in, after they had grazed well.

The rocks around the campsite were carved with symbols and figures, petroglyphs, some a thousand years old.

Du Pré stripped the gear off Walkin' John and Cooter and he put hobbles on the packhorse, who had a habit of taking off for home as soon as he decently could, which meant as soon as he could.

The old horse looked at Du Pré, a little disappointed.

Walkin' John liked the mountains, he would stay even if he got wet.

The old men came riding out of the lodgepole stand, Benetsee in the lead, sitting lightly on his horse, Mukhtar behind, the huge eagle on his arm.

The old Kazakh had an odd hat, one that had a point on the crown and long earflaps.

They rode in.

Benetsee got down, grinning. He went to a stand of alders,

cut a thick one and stripped branches from it, then lopped off
a piece about a foot and a half long. He lashed the crosspiece
to the longer stick and he took a stone and pounded the perch
into the soft earth.

Mukhtar rode up to the T-bar, leaned down, and nudged
the eagle onto it. The huge yellow feet gripped the crosspiece
so hard the bark split.

Then the old man slid down, nimble as a goat.

"Du Pré," said Benetsee, waving the plastic jug of wine, "it
is so good, you bringing us food, tobacco."

"Tobacco is bad for old men," said Du Pré.

Benetsee said something to Mukhtar in the language Du
Pré could not understand.

The old men laughed.

"I brought steaks," said Du Pré. "Enough for the soldiers
too."

"OK," said Benetsee, "you want them to know that. They
are hiding, but they are not very good at it."

Du Pré nodded.

. . . I try to track Benetsee, always find him behind me
laughing, no matter how quiet I am . . .

"Where are they?" said Du Pré.

Benetsee shrugged.

"You know," he said, "they are eating shit out of plastic
sacks; if I wanted them to come, I would cook steaks."

Du Pré laughed.

The sun was still high, there were hours of light left.

He rolled three smokes, lit them, gave one to Benetsee and
one to Mukhtar.

They stood, savoring the good tobacco.

Mukhtar walked away a few feet, put fingers to his lips,
blew a whistling sound so piercing it made Du Pré wince.

Mukhtar said something to Benetsee. Benetsee nodded
and he laughed.

Mukhtar said something else and they laughed again.

Du Pré went to his saddlebags, took out his whiskey, had a big swallow. Another whistle, this time farther up the mountain. Mukhtar whistled again. . . . Idries . . . Du Pré thought.

There was firewood split and seasoned in a rick between two trees. Du Pré built a fire of alder, watched the flames eat the dry wood.

Idries and the other four soldiers padded into the camp. They were all dressed in the tunics and boots and hats of Kazakh herdsmen, all had big packs on their backs. Idries came to Mukhtar, bowed.

The lieutenant walked over.

Mukhtar looked at Chasen, at his short blond hair, his blue eyes. He said something to Idries. Idries laughed.

"He said you looked like a Russian," said Idries. "He has killed a hundred and four Russians . . ."

Chasen looked at the small old man.

"Please tell him I am not a Russian," said Chasen. "A hundred and four. Jesus."

Idries said something to Mukhtar. They both laughed.

The eagle spread its wings, unnerved by all the people suddenly near. Mukhtar went to the huge bird.

He sang something in a low voice and the eagle calmed down.

"Lookit the feet on that bastard," said Mullins. "Christ, look at them claws."

Du Pré found a cast-iron grill under the tent platform. He put more alder wood on the coils and sweet smoke began to curl up from the heat.

"You have mountains like this in Kazakhstan?" said Du Pré to Idries.

"Very much like this," said Idries.

"I would like to see them," said Du Pré.

"Certainly," said Idries.

Du Pré opened the boxes Madelaine had packed and he took out a big plastic bag of steaks and another of rice and peppers. There was a Dutch oven under the platform; he put the rice in it and sat the pot next to the fire.

"Real food," said Mullins.

"That crap they give us," said Sanchez, "keeps you alive but after eating it for days you kinda want to die . . ."

Du Pré offered whiskey, the soldiers shook their heads. Du Pré flopped big steaks on the grill and the searing meat smelled very good.

They ate like starving wolves.

Mukhtar Khan wiped the bloody grease from his chin, he waved his knife, he said something to Idries.

Idries laughed.

Du Pré looked at him.

"He wants to know if you hunt with eagles," said Idries.

Du Pré shook his head.

Mukhtar said something.

Idries nodded.

"He wants to know if you want to come to his home," said Idries. "He offers his hospitality, and if you come he says you can kill Russians with him."

Du Pré laughed.

Mukhtar's face was grave, though.

"Please thank him for me," said Du Pré. "I would very much like to come and kill Russians with him."

Idries spoke to the terrible old man.

Mukhtar Khan looked gravely at Du Pré.

He nodded his head and he put a piece of steak into his mouth.

· Chapter 18 ·

DU PRÉ SAT BACK on Walkin' John; the trail was steep. Cooter whuffled and complained behind them.

Benetsee and Mukhtar with the eagle on his arm were out in front, riding close, side by side. They came through the trees and looked out on the benchlands below. Mukhtar yelled, a high yelp.

He put his heels to his horse's flanks and the gelding dashed forward, the eagle flared her wings a little; Mukhtar turned to take the strain from his shoulder.

Du Pré came out of the trees and he could see the grassy bench-lands below, the main ranch buildings five or so miles away.

A big coyote broke out of a clump of brush and ran toward the round hill to the right.

Mukhtar whooped, reached up and took the hood from the eagle's head, and undid the jesses. The big bird flared, looked round, and as Mukhtar put his horse forward, the eagle spread her wings and she floated up and away.

The eagle circled to get some altitude.

Then she flew toward the coyote, dropped a bit, and rose again. She circled up and up and up, and then she flew off toward the cliff she lived on.

Mukhtar laughed and laughed, putting the hood and jesses in a saddle pouch.

Du Pré rode up to the two old men.

Mukhtar pointed toward the eagle, far away now.

He laughed again. He said something to Benetsee.

Du Pré looked at the old man.

"He said it was a good eagle but still too fat. He fed it too much so it did not want to hunt, it just wanted to go home."

Du Pré nodded.

"How he catch it?" he said to Benetsee.

The old man grinned and shook his head.

"You are too young to know yet," said Benetsee.

They rode down to the ranch's main buildings, and Hoyt Poe came out of the big barn. He had a wide smile on his open face.

"Take your horses?" he said.

. . . He likes horses and they know he does . . . Du Pré thought.

The two old men got down, fished a few things out of the saddlebags, and Benetsee looked at Du Pré.

"You take us, my place," said the old man.

"Some people here," said Du Pré, "want to see Mukhtar Khan."

"We have important business," said Benetsee, "those people wait."

Du Pré shrugged. "I will come back," he said.

"Don't you worry about these horses, Mister Du Pré," said Hoyt.

Du Pré drove down to the county road. Benetsee and Mukhtar Khan sat in the backseat. Benetsee's bent and twisted old hand reached over the seat.

Du Pré sighed.

He stopped the car, got out, fished a half gallon of screw-top wine out of the trunk. He handed it to Benetsee, who laughed.

So did Mukhtar Khan.

. . . I think I kill them both . . . Du Pré thought . . . it is better that way.

He drove slowly along the bench road, took a shortcut through a pasture, drove back west a little.

Benetsee's cabin was open, the door and windows and even the one Du Pré put over the kitchen sink.

The huge dog in front of the cabin, his head turning as Du Pré drove up, did not get up.

Du Pré stopped the car and got out. The dog did wag his docked tail a little.

Pallas appeared in the doorway. She had a headband of red cloth on, and she looked hot and tired.

Benetsee and Mukhtar Khan got out.

"Old goat," said Pallas, "I clean your damn house. I had to use a pitchfork and then a shovel. So you thank me."

"I thank you," said Benetsee.

Mukhtar Khan said something in the language he and Benetsee had been speaking, the one Du Pré could get no sense of.

The big dog got up and came to the old Kazakh and sat, regally.

Mukhtar Khan scratched the big dog's ears.

"You go now," said Benetsee.

Du Pré looked at him.

Benetsee's old wrinkled face split in a smile.

"Mukhtar help her, you go away now," said Benetsee.

Du Pré nodded.

He backed and turned and he drove down the bumpy track to the road.

Madelaine was behind the bar at the Toussaint Saloon, setting beads in soft leather. She had on her bifocals.

Du Pré mixed himself a ditch.

"You seen Pallas?" said Madelaine.

"She is at Benetsee's," said Du Pré. "Those two old men find me, come down, Benetsee says take them to his place. Pallas is there, cleaning."

"Good," said Madelaine, "I drop her off there."

"So why you ask me if I have seen her?" said Du Pré.

"I don't know, her, she stay if I leave her," said Madelaine.

"She had that big damn dog," said Du Pré.

"Berkut?" said Madelaine. "He's a sweetie. He must have come there after I left. He is a strange dog, he is not there and then he is. He keeps an eye on her for sure."

Du Pré laughed.

"You have not met Mukhtar Khan," said Du Pré. "He is as bad as our old friend Benetsee."

"No," said Madelaine, "I have not."

"They tell me to leave," said Du Pré.

Madelaine nodded.

"Benetsee said Pallas is in the wrong place," she said, "so she needs to go to where she should be."

Du Pré looked at her.

"Name me one time that old man is wrong," said Madelaine.

Du Pré shrugged. "She is born here," he said.

"I am not arguing," said Madelaine, "I tell you what Benetsee says."

"OK," said Du Pré.

"So those soldiers, up in the mountains, they are ready, go kill people someplace?" said Madelaine.

"It is what soldiers do," said Du Pré.

"They got people we want dead in Kazakhstan?" said Madelaine.

"I do not know where they are going," said Du Pré.

"I order this movie," said Madelaine, "came today. Put it, the TV."

Du Pré looked at the case. It was covered with ideograms and a picture of a man in a hat like the one Mukhtar Khan wore.

He put it into the player on the wall next to the bar, pressed a couple of buttons.

Strange music.

Ideograms.

A narrator speaking a strange tongue. Then the camera looked out at rolling grassy hills, a lot like parts of Montana.

Riders appeared on the crest of a hill, and then they began to ride down it. There were perhaps fifty of them, men and women, riding easily, moving with the gait of their horses.

Their eyes all looked into the camera. They all sat firmly, loosely, a skill refined. They had no saddles or bridles.

The horses were galloping and dodging bad spots in the earth. The riders came on.

. . . See them with bows and shields and spears . . . Du Pré thought.

"They ride good, Du Pré," said Madelaine.

"Yes," said Du Pré.

"You ride that good?" said Madelaine.

"No," said Du Pré.

Madelaine looked at the riders.

"I have, me, little scared worm in my belly watching them," said Madelaine.

"Me, too," said Du Pré.

"Mukhtar Khan's people," said Madelaine, "Eastern Horde Kazakhs."

"Look," said Du Pré. He pointed at a dog loping along, tongue out, but moving with the horses.

"Looks like Berkut," said Madelaine.

· Chapter 19 ·

"I JUST DON'T see why we cain't come, too," said Sandra.

Little Faith Helen was looking up at her mother, her eyes grave.

"It is too dangerous," said Pidgeon.

"I don't see why a little shoppin' in Billings is dangerous," said Sandra. "I mean, nothing has happened here, has it?"

"The things your mother sent had a small bomb hidden in them," said Pidgeon. "That dangerous enough?"

"A *what*?" said Sandra.

"If you had that thing go off," said Pidgeon, "you'd know it's plenty dangerous."

"What bomb?" said Sandra. "Why'nt you tell me?"

"Sandy," said Hoyt, "I'm just going to be gone a couple of days; when I get back we'll see about shopping."

Sandy nodded.

Hoyt was dressed in neat slacks and a sport coat. He had a small bag in his right hand.

"We need to go," said the man standing next to him. The man had a microphone in his left ear, the cord running down the side of his neck.

Two other men were standing by the big black SUV, looking out at the ranch buildings through their dark glasses. They all had cords on their necks.

Pidgeon looked at the man.

"Anything happens," she said, "I will have your ass nailed to your head."

"Yes, ma'am," said the man. "General La Salle said you would do that."

They both laughed.

Hoyt got in the backseat of the SUV; the three other men got in and the big vehicle moved down the drive.

"I'm sorry," said Sandra, "I'm just goin' nuts here. I wish I was to home."

She went down the steps, a little fast for Faith Helen, who had to jump. She fell and began to cry.

Sandra picked up her daughter. "I'm sorry, sugar," she said, and she walked toward the guesthouse.

Pidgeon shook her head.

She went inside.

Du Pré followed.

"It is pretty hard to protect someone," said Pidgeon, "who won't grasp the danger she is in, that they are all in."

She poured coffee for herself and Du Pré. She lit a filtered cigarette.

"When things get bad," said Pidgeon, "Bart goes and digs a hole someplace. God, I love that man . . ." and she laughed.

"So La Salle calls, they need Hoyt, more testimony," said Du Pré. "I thought he was done."

"Appeals," said Pidgeon. "Most of those bastards shut up and went to prison. Not all of them. Two of them are fighting it . . ."

Du Pré nodded.

"What the Poes should do is take new identities and make new lives," said Pidgeon. "But they come from a tight-knit little town, and they can't let it go. I can't really blame them, but if they won't do anything sensible, there finally isn't a lot anyone can do for them . . ."

"This die down?" said Du Pré.

Pidgeon shrugged. "When you have a bunch of 'true believers' who think Armageddon will bring Jesus back," said Pidgeon, "you aren't speaking of people with a normal complement of humanity in them. I doubt it."

"So what will they do?" said Du Pré. "They will leave here?"

"I suppose," said Pidgeon. "You know, the infiltration of our government by these goddamned fanatics is extensive. It is that sort of time. We'll have better ones, but right now, it ain't good."

Du Pré nodded.

"I've got half a mind to call La Salle and tell him to move the Poes again," said Pidgeon.

"He works good with the horses, works hard on other things," said Du Pré.

"He's not the problem," said Pidgeon. "It's his wife. She just doesn't get it, at all."

"I got to go," said Du Pré. "Madelaine is up at Benetsee's, we are still worried about Pallas."

Pidgeon smiled, nodded.

"She'll be all right," said Pidgeon, "she's tough."

Du Pré went out and down the steps, got into his cruiser, drove toward Benetsee's.

He could hear drumming when he turned and went up the track to the little cabin.

Madelaine was down by the creek and the sweat lodge. Steam curled up in tendrils from the doorway, faint drumming came from the woods.

"They left, Benetsee and the Kazakh," said Madelaine, "said they had things to do, could not wait. Pallas has been in there a long time . . ."

Du Pré nodded.

"Maybe you wait by the porch, Du Pré," said Madelaine. "I will have to get her out of there, a few minutes . . ."

Du Pré walked back up the trail to the front of the cabin.

The huge dog was sprawled on the porch.

Du Pré lit a smoke, scratched the big dog's ears.

Du Pré got up and he went to the side of the cabin and he looked up at the Wolf Mountains.

The eagles weren't there.

. . . Hunting . . .

He went to the car, got some whiskey, rolled another smoke.

Du Pré went back to the porch and he sat down by the dog. The dog's head shot up, he jumped off the porch, and went round the side of the cabin and down toward the sweat lodge.

Du Pré waited.

"Du Pré!" Madelaine yelled. "You come now!"

He walked down the hill.

Pallas and Madelaine were sitting on a log. Pallas's hair was wet, and she had a thick towel in her hands. She lifted it to her head and rubbed.

Du Pré sat on a stump.

The big dog sat at Pallas's feet.

"How you feel?" said Du Pré.

"Pret' good," said Pallas. "I am leaving here though."

"Oh," said Du Pré.

"I talked to Mukhtar Khan," she said. "I mean, I talked to Benetsee. Mukhtar Khan said I belonged where he lives . . ."

"Long way from here," said Du Pré.

Pallas laughed.

"Not so far," she said, "if those two old men speak the same language."

Madelaine rubbed Pallas's back with her left hand.

"You are sure?" said Du Pré.

Pallas nodded. "It is strange," she said.

"When is the last time you eat?" said Madelaine.

Pallas shrugged.

"You come on," said Madelaine, "I will feed you."

They stood up.

Pallas was pale, but her eyes seemed much better.

"We leave you the lodge and fire?" said Madelaine.

"Sure," said Du Pré.

They went up the hill. Du Pré heard the engine of Madelaine's little station wagon start.

He went to the sweat lodge, flipped up the door, pulled out the sheets that covered the floor, spread them over a line. When they were dry, the grass and duff could be brushed away.

He carried water from the creek, put out the pit fires. He split wood for the next time the lodge would be used. He put the ax in the cabin.

Du Pré sat on the porch, smoking. The plains to the south rolled to the horizon, smoky and indistinct.

He got in his old cruiser and drove toward Toussaint.

. . . Maybe I go too . . . he thought . . . but I am too old to learn to ride like they do . . .

· Chapter 20 ·

THE SOLDIERS CAME down from the mountains, jogging easily with heavy packs, and they went into the bunkhouse and then reappeared very quickly.

Du Pré waved to Pidgeon, who was in the kitchen of the main house, from the huge grill he was tending in the backyard. The coals were hot and the boned lamb legs were sitting on a huge steel platter, covered with slices of fresh garlic and lemon, thickly sprinkled with pepper and rosemary.

Du Pré took a big fork and he flopped the meat on the grill. It began to sizzle, and clouds of spiced smoke rose up.

Jack La Salle got out of Du Pré's cruiser, followed by Madelaine.

Madelaine went into the house, La Salle walked toward the soldiers. They stood at attention.

Vandevander saluted, La Salle returned one.

The soldiers were dressed like Kazakh herdsmen; La Salle was in worn hunting clothes, dark green pants, boots, a light shirt with frayed hems, a battered canvas hat.

La Salle and the solders fell to laughing then, and they walked toward Du Pré, who saluted too.

"You want to come back?" said La Salle.

"*Non*," said Du Pré, "I am too old."

"So am I," said La Salle, "but they won't listen."

Du Pré waved his fork at the table filled with liquor, wine, a plastic tub with ice and bottled beer, a platter of cheeses and meats. La Salle went to it, stood behind, took orders, mixed drinks.

Idries sipped soda, and he came and stood by Du Pré.

"I wonder if those old bastards will come," he said. "We are leaving at midnight. And I wish we could have had more time to talk."

"Come back," said Du Pré, "when you do not have to practice living on roots and bark."

"This is much better," said Idries, looking at the meat, on the grill, "and I do hope to come back. Mukhtar Khan may stay for a bit, I suppose. He is so old no one can give him orders."

"Good," said Du Pré, "you leave me both of them. I will probably just shoot them both."

Idries laughed.

"Old men torment younger ones," he said. "It is always so. It is how the military works, of course."

La Salle joined them.

Pidgeon came out of the house with a huge bowl of salad covered in clear plastic, and Madelaine came behind her with a stack of plates, big chargers.

"Where is Bart?" said La Salle. "We surely need to thank him."

"He had to go to Great Falls," said Pidgeon. "Some damn legal thing. Before you go, could you please kill all the lawyers?"

"It might be a better world," said La Salle, "but I doubt it."

"Act local, think global," said Pidgeon. "I mean, you have to start *somewhere* . . ."

Du Pré flipped the meat over, fat side down, and he stood back when flames shot up.

Idries walked out on the gravel lot to a place where he could look at the mountains.

He came back.

"No eagles," he said.

"Maybe they are feeding somewhere," said Du Pré.

"Well," said Idries, "we can hope."

La Salle looked at them.

"Mukhtar Khan caught one of the golden eagles," said Idries. "I have known him all my life, but I don't know how he does it. I have tried to follow him to watch but it is like following water than sinks into the ground . . ."

"The eagle hunters," said La Salle.

"Mukhtar Khan once let me hold an eagle on my arm," said Idries. "I was perhaps twelve. He gave me a guard for my forearm, heavy waxed leather, and then he helped me get the eagle off the perch and on to my left forearm. The bird was hooded. Mukhtar looked at me and I thought I could feel the eagle's eye on me as well, and then the eagle began to grip my arm. I heard the leather creak, felt it start to bend, and the bird kept crushing my arm, and it hurt, and then it hurt more, and I went to my knees, and Mukhtar whistled once and the bird let go . . ."

La Salle and Du Pré looked over their drinks at Idries.

"He got the bird back on the perch and then he said that if I wanted to be an eagle hunter I could not be anything else, if I wished to be good at it, or if I had other aims in my life, he could help me fly eagles he had trained, but I must never try to capture them or teach them how to hunt from the arm . . ."

Idries sipped his soda.

"So I went home and my mother was furious with Mukhtar Khan, for I had bruises on my forearm like black bracelets where the eagle had gripped me, and both bones were fractured, though because I was so young, not all the way. She bound up my arm and she gave me strong tea and then she went to Mukhtar Khan and gave him a piece of her mind. When she came back I asked her what Mukhtar Khan had said, and she was very quiet . . ."

Idries waited while Du Pré turned the meat.

Madelaine brought Du Pré another drink.

"So finally my mother said that Mukhtar Khan told her I would become a soldier, not an eagle hunter, that I was right for that and not for the birds, and my mother, like all mothers, was worried that I would go off and get myself killed . . ."

"So far so good," said La Salle.

They all laughed.

"You should come," said Idries, looking at Du Pré. "We have some work to do . . ."

Du Pré nodded. "I come when I can."

Sandra and little Faith Helen appeared, walking slowly round the house.

The beautiful little child looked at the strange men in their strange dress and she smiled shyly.

Pidgeon went to them, took Faith Helen's other hand, led them to the drinks table, got a soda for Sandra and one for the little girl.

"He's testifying again," said Du Pré, looking at La Salle.

La Salle nodded. He looked sad.

"In a country such as this . . ." he said, "there are good times and bad ones. This is a very bad one indeed."

"You see Pallas?" said Madelaine, looking at Du Pré.

Du Pré shook his head.

"She has been gone two or three days," said Madelaine, "took Moondog and off she went, she told her mother not to worry about her . . ."

. . . Pallas . . . Du Pré thought . . . Is she up there? She knows how to live . . .

"If she don't show up by tomorrow . . ." said Madelaine, looking at Du Pré.

"Benetsee is looking after her," said Du Pré.

"We did not see either of the old men or the young woman," said Idries.

The meat was ready and they ate then, dripping slices of spiced lamb, rice, salad, good crusty bread. The soldiers had been famished. The food was so good everyone ate far too much.

It was still light and would be for a while.

Idries and Du Pré and Madelaine strolled down toward the big barn, to check on the horses.

The Wolf Mountains were shadowed, light from the westering sun marking black on the deep green, gray, and white.

Du Pré squinted at the mountains, saw movement. Three riders.

They came out of the trees, riding flat out, and the horses jumped over the upper fence and landed and ran on. The riders came to the gate on the up side of the big pasture, and Benetsee got down and he opened the swing gate and Mukhtar Khan and Pallas rode on through.

Mukhtar Khan had an eagle on his wrist and Pallas had another on hers. The three rode hard straight for Du Pré and Madelaine and Idries.

Du Pré walked up to the fence, swung open the big gate, and in a moment the three riders came through.

Pallas was laughing. She rode in a circle round Du Pré and Idries and Madelaine. Then she stopped and she pulled the hood from the eagle, which flared and began to beat its wings.

Pallas flung the bird up and the eagle dipped and rose up, huge wings pumping.

Mukhtar Khan set his free, too.

The big birds circled, going up and up.

Pallas slid down from Moondog.

She looked at Idries, Madelaine, and Du Pré.

"I am going home, my new home, maybe in a few months," she said.

She looked at the Wolf Mountains, maybe saying good-bye.

· **Chapter 21** ·

DU PRÉ AND MADELAINE and Jacqueline and Pallas and Lourdes sat at the kitchen table.

. . . My father Catfoot's house . . . Du Pré thought . . . then it was mine and now it is Jacqueline's.

Jacqueline held her face tight but her eyes were glistening. "You are sure?" she said. "You are going there? It is on the other side of the world."

Pallas smiled. She looked radiant.

"I am sure," she said. "Bart will take me there when I am ready."

"To stay," said Jacqueline.

"I don't belong here anymore," said Pallas. "I go to that school, the East, I learn mathematics, I learn physics, I learn a lot about those things, go someplace else, think, make a lot of money, and I don't belong there either. You have seen me, *maman*. You have seen me, I am so sad I want to die . . ."

Jacqueline nodded.

"OK," she said, "they got mail, telephones there maybe."

"They do," said Pallas.

Jacqueline looked at Du Pré. Du Pré nodded.

"I am following Granpère's songs maybe," said Pallas.

"Following his songs?" said Jacqueline. "Songs, him, come from France."

"Some don't," said Pallas. "Some come from the sweat."

"Those songs," said Jacqueline.

Raymond came in, tired, dressed in his lineman's clothes.

"She is going to the other side of the earth," said Jacqueline. "Maybe we never see her again."

Raymond nodded. He went to the fridge and he got a beer and he opened it and he drank.

"She is doing what she wants," he said, "since she was two maybe. I got her footprints on my head. I got lots of them, you too. She wants to go there, she is going. . . . But not for a while so she has time to think."

He smiled at his daughter.

She got up and they hugged.

Du Pré stood and so did Madelaine.

"She is not going tonight," said Jacqueline, and she cried. Pallas went to her, hugged her.

"I have to do this, *maman*," she said.

She kissed her father and her mother. "I will go in a while, not for a couple months at least . . ."

She went off to the addition where the younger children either slept or beat the crap out of each other, depending.

"She was so unhappy," said Raymond, "if she goes somewhere she thinks is right, she will maybe not be so sad . . ."

Jacqueline nodded.

Pallas came back, looked at Raymond and Jacqueline. "They are animals . . ." she said.

"All you got to say?" said Jacqueline.

"Lourdes is my size," said Pallas. "She is wearing the rest of my things."

They all walked out to Du Pré's cruiser.

They got in and Pallas was smiling, a smile Du Pré had never seen before. He drove out to Bart's, where two SUVs were idling.

Bart came to the car, looked into the dinged old heap.

"Are you coming?" he said to Pallas.

She shook her head and got out of the car.

"When she comes," said Idries, "Mukhtar Khan will have prepared for her arrival, will look for an eagle for her and a rifle to kill Russians with."

The old Kazakh shaman was sitting in a shadow, almost invisible. He stood up. He said something, Idries bent to hear him, nodding.

Berkut, the huge dog, padded up to Pallas and he sat; she put her hand on his head.

Idries looked at Pallas. "Berkut has found his person," he said. "He would be too unhappy going home without her. As will I," he added softly.

Berkut rumbled something deep in his chest. He leaned against Pallas.

"We had best go," said Idries. "You will come when you can?"

"Yes," said Pallas, "I will come as soon as I can."

Bart and the soldiers and Mukhtar Khan got into the SUVs, and the little convoy pulled away and rolled down the long drive to the county road. Pallas walked out to the barn and the horses.

"She will be going next time," said Benetsee, appearing from nowhere.

Du Pré looked at him.

"You got wine, anyone?" said Benetsee. The old man was wearing Mukhtar Khan's hat and embroidered vest.

"So you are here old bastard, watching?" said Madelaine, "cannot say good-bye even?"

"Did that," said Benetsee. "About that wine now."

Du Pré went to his old cruiser, fished a jug of screw-top out of the trunk.

Benetsee drank a lot, wiped his mouth.

"What you know about all this?" said Du Pré.

"I want a smoke," said Benetsee. "I am tired, explaining things. You open your eyes, I don't have to so much."

Du Pré rolled a smoke, handed it to Benetsee.

"I am so glad," said Du Pré, "you did not send the eagles with that other old bastard."

Benetsee laughed. "Mukhtar Khan said they were pret' sorry eagles, pret' small, not like his, weigh twice as much. Said they would be too small, hunt wolves."

"Christ," said Du Pré, "we can't even have decent eagles."

"Pallas, she is going to be all right?" said Madelaine, glaring at Benetsee.

"Strange times, you know," said Benetsee, "people can move all over the earth very fast, but it is not good for most of them I think. They don't know where they are, don't care, Earth don't speak to them . . ."

"You are not answering, my question," said Madelaine, "and I want a good answer."

"Pallas, she stay here," said Benetsee, "she have time now to say good-bye, here, and then she is fine."

Du Pré looked at Benetsee.

"I hope you are right," said Du Pré.

They went to the Toussaint Saloon and found that Bassman and Père Godin had come without letting anyone know they were planning to. They had the amps and stands onstage, the two mikes for Du Pré.

He went to his cruiser and got the old fiddle case Catfoot had made seventy years ago, and the fiddle that Du Pré loved best. It was old and glowing and Catfoot had had it first and then Du Pré, and the very dark instrument carried a memory of millions of notes played on it.

Catfoot had told Du Pré never to take the fiddle to play at a big festival.

"It is too good a fiddle for a poor Métis," said Catfoot. "I found it in Europe, the war. Very good fiddle."

Du Pré played for the first time in weeks, and the crowd in the bar grew.

Pidgeon came in with Pallas and the Poes, and the little girl got a bright red soda with a tiny umbrella in it.

Hoyt and Sandra danced and the music held them close and they held each other and for a little time were safe in beauty.

Hoyt was spirited away once again the next morning, to testify again, this time at a secret hearing in Washington.

Sandra cried as the escorts, big men in dark suits that were pretty lumpy, led Hoyt to the car.

Hoyt just looked sad as he walked away.

· Chapter 22 ·

"THEY GOT BACK to Kazakhstan just fine," said Jack La Salle, "no problems, and Idries took Mukhtar Khan home. I gather Pallas is convinced she belongs there and plans to go as soon as possible."

"Yah," said Du Pré, "Idries's wife and children were killed while ago, they were in a plane went down. He has been a lonely man. Pallas and Idries found each other and made a choice. Madelaine saw it, I didn't."

"Well," said La Salle, "Poe should be able to come home tomorrow. His testimony is over, but a lot of people still want him dead. I think our best bet for keeping him safe is indirection. I plan to get him on a commercial flight from Washington to Spokane. You know the drill, much flap about secrecy, and then send it regular mail."

"OK," said Du Pré.

"You pick him up there," said La Salle.

Du Pré sighed. "OK," he said, "when?"

La Salle gave him the flight number and arrival time. "It's hard to tell what to expect," said La Salle. "Temple Security wants Poe dead, and they'll do it if they can. Of that I am certain. But I'm also certain they won't take out a whole planeload of people to do it."

"OK," said Du Pré, "but I think Bart's people do this better than I do."

"Foote wouldn't sign off on it," said La Salle. "All his security people are on other details. He sounded regretful . . ."

"You are not setting me up," said Du Pré.

"Du Pré," said La Salle, "things are so bad all I can say is that I hope not. Believe me, if I knew a better way I'd do it."

"Ver' bad," said Du Pré.

"I love my country," said La Salle, "but this is very bad."

Du Pré put the telephone back on the hook. He drove down to the Toussaint Saloon and he parked and went in.

Madelaine was sitting on her stool behind the bar. There were a couple of ranchers there, drinking beers and arguing about horses.

"I got to go to Spokane," said Du Pré.

"Pick up Poe," said Madelaine, "they won't bring him back here?"

Du Pré shook his head.

"La Salle said he would send Poe on a regular plane," said Du Pré. "He sounded worried, said that was the best he could do."

"I go too," said Madelaine. "I call Susan."

Du Pré went into the kitchen and he made some sandwiches and he put them in a little soft cooler, along with a bottle of pink fizzy wine for Madelaine.

He went out to his old cruiser.

Susan Klein came round the corner of the saloon.

"Du Pré," she said, "Pallas is really moving to the other side of the earth?"

"Yah," Du Pré said, slowly shaking his head.

Madelaine came out.

"See you, I guess," said Susan. "Anyone in there?"

"Bud and Charley," said Madelaine, "arguing about quarter horses."

"They've been doing that," said Susan, "since about 1980."

Du Pré started the cruiser, and he heard a clunk. The engine died.

"Oh, boy," said Madelaine.

"Shit," said Du Pré.

"Take my car," said Madelaine, "go to Bart's, get one of the Suburbans."

They drove by the gas station next door.

"It went," said Du Pré. He pointed back at the old cruiser. The mechanic nodded.

Then they went on.

They parked next to Bart's machine shed and Du Pré and Madelaine got out and moved a few things to get to one of the big green Suburbans.

Sandra and little Faith Helen waved from the main house, and they walked quickly over.

"You goin' to get Hoyt?" said Sandra. "We are comin'. . ."

Madelaine looked at Du Pré.

He sighed and nodded.

When he and Madelaine got back into the Suburban, Madelaine grinned at him.

Du Pré looked at the ceiling.

They drove to the main highway and then headed west, finally coming to the interstate not far from Missoula.

Little Faith Helen was silent. Sandra hummed tunes from the country music station she listened to.

They stopped at a rest stop, walked a bit, went on.

Du Pré had a slug of whiskey.

"I really wish you wouldn't do that," said Sandra. "I mean, you ain't supposed to, Mister Du Pré."

Madelaine looked at her.

"Du Pré," she said, "go back, that first exit."

Du Pré drove over the freeway and he headed back east and then he went south on a broad boulevard lined with shopping malls.

"Here," said Madelaine.

Du Pré pulled into a giant parking lot.

"Now you," said Madelaine, looking at Sandra, "are a pain in the ass. You get out here, you shop, we will stop at that coffee shop for you, the way back . . ."

Sandra looked horrified. "That'll be hours," she whined.

"Then shut up and act right," said Madelaine. "Any more crap, you, you get dropped off, money for a bus ticket, we don't stop the way back. So what will it be here?"

"OK, OK," said Sandra, "I'm sorry."

"People are helping, you don't bitch," said Madelaine.

Faith Helen looked at her mother, wide-eyed.

They went on.

Spokane appeared suddenly, and Du Pré took the airport exit. He made his way to the terminal, and he stopped while Sandra and Faith Helen got out.

"We will be right over there," said Madelaine, pointing to the parking lot. "You meet him, come over there so we are not driving in circles."

Sandra and the little girl got out.

"Flight 487," said Du Pré, "Delta."

A police car behind them flashed its headlights, and Du Pré drove off.

"She is a real pain in the ass," said Madelaine.

"Yah," said Du Pré.

"Sorry I lose my temper, her," said Madelaine.

"Good," said Du Pré, laughing. "I would have said no, the ranch."

"It is my fault," said Madelaine, "I was being kind."

Planes were coasting out of the sky now and again.

Du Pré looked at his watch.

"Should be here, not long," he said. He rolled a smoke, lit it, gave it to Madelaine for her one puff.

"I think Pallas is OK now," said Madelaine.

"Yah," said Du Pré.

"She is a strange kid," said Madelaine, "genius, but doesn't want what that could bring her. So what does she do in Kazakhstan?"

"Learns to ride like they do," said Du Pré.

"No wonder, then," said Madelaine. "I go there myself, I learn to ride like that."

A jet plane's engines screamed, roared, then the sound lessened and they could see the plane rising steeply into the sky.

Then Hoyt and Sandra and little Faith Helen came out of the terminal, and Sandra pointed toward Du Pré and Madelaine.

The little family walked toward the Suburban and they all were smiling.

They loaded up and drove to a restaurant, a fairly nice one, and had something to eat. Hoyt was famished and Du Pré and Madelaine laughed to see how quickly he finished his meal.

They had desserts and got back on the road.

It was a long drive to Toussaint, and they would not get there before dark.

· Chapter 23 ·

THERE WAS HIGHWAY construction on the eastbound lanes not far out of Spokane. They sat in traffic for a few minutes, and then they passed the flagman and were able to speed up.

They drove on, over the Idaho border with Montana, and down a long slope.

Hoyt was dozing, exhausted.

"I need a bathroom," said Sandra. She was holding little Faith Helen on her lap, and the child was holding a big doll, one with eyes that opened when it was set upright.

There was a rest area a few miles on. Sandra went into the restrooms, and Hoyt woke up.

"You need to go?" he said to Faith Helen.

The child shook her head.

Sandra came back and got in.

It was hot out and the AC had decided not to work. The windows were all rolled down, and Du Pré backed and turned and started down the long, bumpy return lane. The grass on the verges hadn't been cut in a while, either.

Little Faith Helen held her doll up to the open window. The Suburban hit a bump and the doll flew out the window.

Du Pré saw the doll go into the tall grass.

Faith Helen started screaming.

"You quit that!" Sandra yelled. Faith Helen began to sob.

"Could we get the doll?" said Hoyt, leaning close to Du Pré's ear.

Du Pré backed up to a place near where he thought the doll had fallen.

Hoyt got out and he looked in the grass.

"Let's help," said Madelaine.

Du Pré put the transmission in park and he got out and he and Madelaine went to Hoyt, and then Du Pré walked back toward the rest area parking lot while Madelaine and Hoyt walked the other way.

They searched through the tall rank grass. It was thick, bunched at the base.

"Dang it," said Hoyt, "I am sorry for this."

They continued searching.

Madelaine was now well ahead of the parked Suburban. Hoyt was perhaps twenty feet from the back and Du Pré was a good hundred feet past him.

Du Pré started forward.

There was a flash and then a terrible red bloom that engulfed the Suburban. Hoyt screamed and ran toward the vehicle, but the blast blew him off his feet and back.

Du Pré pulled him away.

Madelaine was running toward Du Pré.

The fire was so hot and fast everything in the body caught and blazed. Black smoke rose, and the heat was so intense the grass caught fire.

Hoyt was screaming and again tried to crawl toward the inferno.

Du Pré hit him in the back of the neck and he grabbed his feet and pulled him away.

Madelaine knelt beside Hoyt.

Hoyt was moaning.

The Suburban was a blackened lump of twisting metal.

Du Pré looked down at his feet.

Traffic on the interstate slowed, then went on. A Highway Patrol car came speeding into the rest area.

It stopped by Du Pré and Madelaine and Hoyt Poe. The officer was speaking into his radio.

He got out. "Jesus," said the cop. "What happened?"

"It blew up," said Du Pré.

"You got out though," said the cop.

"My wife and baby din't," Hoyt screamed, "they din't, they din't."

"Oh my God," said the cop. He grabbed his radio.

The fire in the grass was licking at the trees. Some of the lower branches were smoking and soon would flame.

Sirens.

A few minutes later fire trucks and four ambulances had arrived, and they soon got the grass and trees sprayed down.

The Suburban now just smoldered, heat rising from it in rippling waves.

Du Pré and Madelaine and Poe were put in the backseat of a patrol car.

Hoyt sat staring out of the window, his face slack.

. . . If we were in there we would all be dead . . . Du Pré thought. . . . I will have blood for this . . .

The first cop came and he opened the back door and Du Pré and Madelaine got out.

Another cop, older, with the flat eyes of a man who had seen too many people do too many bad things, came over.

"Well," he said, "what the hell happened here?"

Du Pré looked at him.

"Call this number," said Du Pré, "ask for La Salle."

The officer looked at Du Pré. "And why," he said, "should I do that?"

"He has to know," said Du Pré.

"Has to know?" said the cop.

Du Pré nodded.

"And what is this La Salle supposed to tell me?" said the cop.

Du Pré leaned close to the man's ear. "The young man in the car over there is a witness in a very big case and somebody just tried to kill him," said Du Pré. "You call La Salle and maybe you don't get the FBI and ATF and the rest here."

The cop nodded.

He walked off and he punched in the numbers into his cell phone. He waited, said something, said something else, then he spoke. He listened nodding. He motioned for Du Pré and handed him the phone.

"Oh, God," said La Salle, "I am sorry."

"You did your best," said Du Pré.

"The little girl?" said La Salle.

"She and Sandy did not make it," said Du Pré.

"Bastards," said La Salle.

"So," said Du Pré.

"They'll have to interview you all," said La Salle. "I will get there as soon as I can."

"Where are you taking us?" said Du Pré to the cop.

"Missoula," he said.

"Missoula," said Du Pré into the cell phone.

"I'm on my way," said La Salle. "God, Du Pré, I am so sorry."

Du Pré rolled a smoke.

He lit it, gave it to Madelaine.

"I don't got ID," said Madelaine, "it was in the Suburban. So maybe I end up in that prison in Cuba."

Hoyt had started to scream again. He pounded on the windows of the patrol car.

"I'll put you in with Lindemann," said the cop. "Your friend needs a hospital, I think."

A couple of ambulance attendants went to the Highway Patrol car where Hoyt continued to scream.

"We stay with him," said Du Pré.

The cop looked at him. "That bad?" he said.

Du Pré nodded.

"What is this all about?" said the cop.

"La Salle will tell you, he will be in Missoula soon," said Du Pré.

The cop nodded. "OK," he said.

The EMTs gave Hoyt a shot of something.

Madelaine and Du Pré got in the backseat with him.

The cop drove down past the burnt Suburban and into the traffic.

Madelaine hugged Du Pré's arm.

· Chapter 24 ·

DU PRÉ AND MADELAINE and Hoyt sat in the back of a laundry van, behind a pile of bags full of soiled linens that smelled of the Missoula jail. The van turned and accelerated and turned and slowed and finally stopped.

The back doors opened and Du Pré got out, held out his hand for Madelaine. Hoyt unfolded and stood, a bit unsteadily. His eyes were glassy from the sedatives he had been given.

Pidgeon was waiting with another of the Suburbans.

Du Pré and Madelaine got in, Hoyt climbed on to a mattress in the back and he curled up.

"You drive," said Pidgeon to Du Pré.

Du Pré nodded, started the engine, backed out of the parking space. He went down the ramp and out on to a busy street, turned right, right again. They went down the expressway for a few miles and then they turned off onto another highway, a two-lane that went far north of the main route.

As soon as the road opened up Du Pré felt under the seat, found a bottle of whiskey, had some. There was tobacco, too. He rolled a smoke and he gave the cigarette to Madelaine.

"Thanks," said Du Pré.

"Christ," said Pidgeon, "it's only luck you're alive. I'm as angry as I ever been in my life . . ."

Du Pré jerked his head back toward Hoyt Poe. They rode for hours then in silence.

When they got to Bart and Pidgeon's house, Du Pré parked. He opened the back of the Suburban and Poe slid out, blinking. He yawned. Du Pré walked him to the guesthouse. Poe looked at Du Pré for a moment, then he nodded and he went inside and he shut the door.

Du Pré walked back to the main house, up the back steps, and into the kitchen.

Pidgeon was in her office, looking at her computer screen. She typed something. She waited. She typed some more.

She got up from the chair.

Madelaine was in the kitchen, making some sandwiches.

"The TV people are all over this," said Pidgeon, "and that little prince of the FBI upon whose patch the crime was done is being very . . . unpleasant . . ."

"I know," said Du Pré. "He has ver' bad manners."

"You don't make that man happy," said Madelaine.

"*Non*," said Du Pré.

"You're lucky they didn't try to hold you as a material witness," said Pidgeon.

Du Pré shrugged.

"So," said Pidgeon, "what did happen? I take it you said little if anything to the folks there."

"The car blew up," said Du Pré.

Pidgeon looked at him.

"We went to a restaurant and somebody followed us," said Madelaine. "That was the only time that there was nobody in the truck, only then."

"Temple must have had somebody at the airport," said Pidgeon.

"These people are evil," said Madelaine, "truly evil."

"Cops wanted us to say who we thought did it," said Du Pré.

"And you just stonewalled them?" said Pidgeon.

"I call Foote," said Madelaine, "who calls some lawyer in Missoula, and after that, we are in the laundry truck pret' quick. Hoyt is so ill he can't take care of himself, so we all come back here."

"They are fighting among themselves," said Du Pré, "cops, FBI, ATF, all fighting. Explosion happens in Montana, but Spokane is nearer. I am ready to help but then they threaten me, do the authority thing, you know, and I don't like that . . ."

"That crap," said Pidgeon. "Oh, Harvey will have a good time with this one."

Du Pré nodded.

"It won't be long before the TV people are here," said Pidgeon. "What do you want to do?"

"Nothing," said Du Pré. "They are here, then whoever is trying to kill Poe won't come."

Pidgeon nodded.

She looked out the window. Hoyt was going into the big barn.

"Du Pré," said Pidgeon, "he went into the barn."

Du Pré put on his hat and he walked out the back door and through the stand of birches to the big gravel lot and across it to the barn. He went inside.

Poe was raking and cleaning one of the stalls.

He looked up when Du Pré came in.

"I have to work," he said.

"OK," said Du Pré, "no ATV, no tractor though."

"No," said Poe, "I won't do that. God. What will I tell Sandy's mama? I just want to work for a while. If I work hard, takes my mind off things."

"OK," said Du Pré, "there is plenty to do here. Also you can dig the rest of that trench where the bad footing is, the north side."

Du Pré walked back to the house.

"He needs to do something," said Du Pré. "Where is Booger Tom?"

"He went off to buy horses," said Pidgeon. "Wyoming some place."

The telephone rang. Pidgeon answered it.

Du Pré turned on the TV.

"The police have several suspects in the terrible explosion that claimed the lives of an American soldier's wife and child . . ."

"Electronic age," said Pidgeon. "That should have them shitting bricks in Spokane. Really shitting bricks. It didn't take Harvey more'n about twenty minutes to get that on the air, worldwide . . ."

Then there was footage of the blackened Suburban, the trucks around it, evidence technicians now, from the FBI.

"Tell me again how it went up," said Pidgeon. "Just a big red bloom of flame?"

"Yah," said Du Pré.

Pidgeon went to her study, tapped a few things into her computer. She came back with a printed sheet of paper.

The thing pictured was a short cylinder with two magnets on its sides, flat to the top.

"Kinda standard terrorist stuff," said Pidgeon. "Clap that on the gas tank and it blows a hole in the tank with a hot column of gas. Instant boom."

"Who makes them?" said Du Pré.

"Everybody. Anybody," said Pidgeon. "Simple, get a little battery and timer, set that, slap it on the tank, good to go. A bright high school student could easily make one up."

"Oh, good," said Du Pré.

"You don't teach in a high school," said Pidgeon, "you got nothing to worry about. Anyway, it must have been set to go off an hour later after you left the restaurant. That'd give you time to get on the road if Hoyt and Sandy had needed to stop somewhere, pick up something. So, you just happened to be out of the vehicle."

Du Pré nodded.

"You see anything in the restaurant parking lot?" said Pidgeon.

Du Pré shook his head.

"Damn," said Pidgeon.

"Du Pré and me, thought it was safe," said Madelaine.

"So," said Pidgeon, "somebody found out Poe was flying to Spokane and somebody called somebody."

"La Salle was keeping it quiet, I thought," said Du Pré.

"So did he," said Pidgeon, "so Temple had help."

"Help?" said Du Pré.

"This administration," said Pidgeon, "is past belief."

"I wish we didn't have to believe it," said Du Pré.

· Chapter 25 ·

DU PRÉ FOUND HOYT sitting on a bench near the hole he was digging to repair the footing. He had his face in his hands. Du Pré sat down next to him; he rolled a smoke.

"I'm sorry," said Hoyt. "I'll get back to work in a minute." He had blisters on his hands, leaking blood.

"There will be six security people, here, Bart's, later tonight or in the morning," said Du Pré.

"Too late," said Hoyt, "all this is too late."

"You got to eat something," said Du Pré. "Here." He handed Hoyt a sandwich and a can of pop.

Hoyt unwrapped the food, took a bite, chewed. "Got no spit," he said, dropping the chewed wad into his hand and then tossing it into the hole. He threw the sandwich in after.

"You stop work now, clean up your hands. They give you some pills, take some, sleep," said Du Pré.

"I don't think I will ever sleep again, Mister Du Pré," said Hoyt.

"Come on," said Du Pré. He stood up and so did Hoyt and they walked to the guesthouse.

"I go in there and Sandy's stuff and Faith Helen's stuff is there like they'll be back any minute and they ain't never comin' back at all," said Hoyt. "How'd this happen? God, God, I join up, I want to help my country, I do what they tell me to do, I try to, and now Sandy's dead of it and so is Faith Helen. They was killed, Mister Du Pré, because I tried to do the right things. I told what those Temple advisers were doin', what their boss, that Lloyd Cutler, knew they were doin'. I knew it would be kinda hard to do and Sandy, Sandy said *well the Lord would want you to* and we prayed and prayed, Mister Du Pré, and this is how God answers prayers . . ."

Du Pré led Hoyt inside the house, found the pill bottle, and handed two to Hoyt. Hoyt ran the tap, rinsed his hands, drew a glass of water, and he swallowed the pills.

They went back outside.

The sun was now behind the mountains and plains to the west, though it would be light for a while.

A truck engine sounded on the drive and Du Pré looked through a gap in the trees and in a moment a dusty pickup truck passed. It was not one Du Pré knew.

Hoyt sat slumped against the porch rail.

He yawned. "These damn pills make me sleepy but I won't never sleep again."

A young man came walking up the path to the guesthouse. He was tall and loose-limbed; he wore faded western clothes, a shirt with the sleeves ripped off at the shoulder, and a crumpled straw hat smudged with oil and dust.

He came up to the porch.

"Hoyt?" he said.

Hoyt looked up. "Bobby Don?" he said. "Whatcha doin' here?"

"Come to see you," said the young man. "Drove up and didn't stop."

Du Pré stood up.

"They's dead, Bobby Don," said Hoyt.

"I know," said the young man. "I know."

Bobby Don looked at Du Pré. "I'm his cousin," he said. "That lady at the house, the purty one, made me show her m' driver's license. Glad Hoyt and m' daddy's last name's the same. She done patted me down too . . ."

"It is a bad time," said Du Pré.

"God," said Hoyt. He and his cousin hugged.

"Hoyt," said Bobby Don, "whyn't you and me go down the roadhouse and have some drinks and git some food in ya . . ."

Hoyt nodded.

"*Non,*" said Du Pré, "it is too dangerous."

"It's been plenty dangerous and you ain't done shit that I can see," said Bobby Don, "an' what I know, I think it'll be just fine tonight and maybe not so good tomorrow."

He reached up to push his hat off his forehead. He had a Marine Corps tattoo on the back of his right hand.

"OK," said Du Pré.

He went into the house, got the bottle of pills. He brought it back out.

"He's had two of these, shouldn't drink much," said Du Pré.

Bobby Don looked at them.

"Two beers and maybe Hoyt'll sleep," he said.

"Be careful," said Du Pré. He walked back to the main house.

Pidgeon was sitting on the porch with Madelaine.

"You met his cousin," said Pidgeon.

Du Pré nodded.

"Cousin's got some good sense," said Pidgeon. "He called, said he was coming, said when he was coming, and said he had ID and that Hoyt would recognize him. I checked anyway. Bobby Don's only been out of the marines for three months."

Du Pré looked at her.

"They aren't giving out many medals in this war," said Pidgeon, "but Bobby Don has one. A Silver Star. Any other war, it would have been the Medal of Honor."

. . . Yes, this war . . . Du Pré thought.

"Good that he came," said Madelaine.

"He'll be good for Hoyt," said Pidgeon. "My God, what that boy has been through."

Hoyt and Bobby Don walked past, Bobby Don waved while Hoyt looked carefully at the ground. They got into the dusty pickup with the little camper and the Texas license plates.

Bobby Don held the door open for Hoyt, shut it when his cousin got in, and then he got in and the truck moved down the drive, turning toward Toussaint when he got to the county road.

Du Pré yawned.

"Me, too," said Madelaine. "We go sleep, your cabin. We did not sleep last night, all those questions."

Du Pré shook his head. "What you tell them?" he said.

"I tell them the Suburban blew up," said Madelaine. "For a while they seemed to think I blew it up."

"Christ," said Pidgeon.

Du Pré and Madelaine stood up.

"Sweet dreams," said Pidgeon.

Du Pré and Madelaine walked to the little cabin Du Pré stayed in from time to time.

It had his old fiddles and tapes, and some of Catfoot's things, some pictures.

Catfoot had come back from Europe with four Luger pistols, some German decorations, a Schmeisser machine pistol, and an eighteenth-century apothecary's balance, one with tiny brass weights and an elaborately filigreed stand.

Du Pré waited while Madelaine showered and then he did and by the time he came to bed Madelaine was sound asleep.

Du Pré felt restless. He took a bottle of whiskey outside and he sat while the light failed.

At deepest dusk a pale coyote crossed the field below the cabin, dashing from one wrinkle in the earth to another. The nightjars swooped and dipped around the light on the high pole, eating insects that fluttered in the glow.

Du Pré drank some whiskey, looked up at the stars.

. . . What has my country come to . . . he thought . . . this has happened before, but never this bad . . .

Du Pré rolled a smoke.

He went inside, quietly, and he got a fiddle from the cabinet, one Catfoot had made. It was crude and the top was too thick, but it had a surprisingly lively tone.

Du Pré went back outside and shut the cabin door.

He tuned the fiddle, tuned the bow, pulled dead hairs away. He drew the bow across the strings. He played a little of "Baptiste's Lament."

. . . Pallas is going all the way on the other side of the world, she will be riding fast with an eagle on her arm. With that big dog loping along beside her horse . . . Hoyt Poe travels a road no one should have to go . . .

Du Pré fiddled some scales.

. . . There will be a big moon later . . .

He yawned, stretched, and he had a little more whiskey and another smoke.

It was chilly, cold air was sliding down the mountain wall.

He went in, put the fiddle away, undressed, got into the bed. It was warm and smelled of Madelaine, the herbs she put in the soap that she made.

Du Pré fell down and down into the soft dark. Slept.

Chapter 26

DU PRÉ STIRRED, OPENED his eyes, looked at the window. It was light out, dawn had come a while ago.

He heard a tap on the door.

He got up, pulled on his pants, went to the door. Madelaine murmured in her sleep.

Pidgeon was standing there.

"Damn it," she said softly, "Hoyt and his cousin aren't here. I don't think that they came back last night . . ."

Du Pré nodded. He went back into the cabin to get dressed.

Madelaine woke, saw him pulling on his clothes.

"Hoyt and his cousin, not here," said Du Pré.

"Oh," said Madelaine. "Oh, God."

Du Pré sat on the bed, pulled on his boots.

"Du Pré," said Madelaine.

"I see about it," said Du Pré.

He went out. Pidgeon was sitting in her sedan waiting. She drove fast to Toussaint. The saloon was not yet open.

The truck with the Texas plates wasn't there.

"What do you think?" said Pidgeon.

Du Pré looked over at the little gas station and garage. His old car was parked beside the building, front end to the street.

Pidgeon followed his gaze. She drove to the old cruiser.

Du Pré got out, went to the trunk. It had been jimmied; the lock was bent and the lid would not close. Du Pré sighed. He lifted the lid.

The .50-caliber sniper rifle was gone, so was the ammunition canister.

Pidgeon came over to him. "Oh my God," she said.

Du Pré nodded.

"You don't have the plate numbers on the cousin's truck . . . ?" said Pidgeon.

Du Pré shook his head.

"What do you think?" said Pidgeon.

Du Pré looked up at the mountains.

"I think," he said, "we better find them."

Pidgeon nodded.

She looked at her watch.

Susan Klein came out of the saloon and she began sweeping the long boardwalk porch.

Pidgeon drove over and got out.

Du Pré checked the rest of the cruiser. The two thousand dollars he kept under the dash was gone. Also the heavy flashlight and the Glock, the spare magazines and cartridges. Water jug, cooler.

Pidgeon returned. "They came in and the cousin made a telephone call," said Pidgeon, "they had a couple of drinks and then they ate burgers. They left. Susan said Hoyt looked bad . . ."

"They are going to kill somebody," said Du Pré, "but I don't know who it is. Hoyt, he had sniper training."

"So did Bobby Don," said Pidgeon. "OK, they have eleven or so hours on us. They could be anywhere within, say, seven hundred miles of here . . ."

Du Pré nodded.

"I better call Harvey," said Pidgeon.

Du Pré looked at her.

"You talk to Harvey," said Du Pré, "then Harvey has to do something. And if they are on their way to Washington, they have that rifle, they will spend the rest of their lives in prison."

Pidgeon nodded. "You're right. And we don't know for sure what they mean to do," she said. "Other 'n kill somebody."

"Yah," said Du Pré.

"Who do you think they blame for this?" said Pidgeon.

Du Pré lifted his palms skyward. "Everyone, Temple Security? Just Lloyd Cutler? Who knows?"

"I can see about Bobby Don Poe," said Pidgeon, "maybe get a little help finding his truck."

"They may not be in it," said Du Pré, "got rid of it by now."

"If we do find it," said Pidgeon, "and they are in it, well, OK, what then?"

Du Pré shook his head.

"That guy Cutler, owns Temple Security, he lives in Dallas, I think," said Pidgeon. "Maybe they'll head there."

"Maybe," said Du Pré.

"But what if Hoyt just wanted out of here, wanted to go home," said Pidgeon.

"Then he doesn't need the rifle," said Du Pré. "He is an honest man, why he got into such trouble, but I think has cut loose now. He thinks he will die, so it does not matter . . ."

Pidgeon nodded.

"I do have to let Harvey know," she said.

Du Pré nodded. He went into the gas station, paid his bill, went out to the old cruiser. He took a fencing hammer from the trunk and he banged the loop back far enough so the trunk lid would close.

He drove back out to Bart and Pidgeon's.

Madelaine was in the kitchen. She had made a huge breakfast, eggs and cheese and chilies and fresh popovers.

Du Pré wolfed the food down, he drank coffee.

"Got nothing on Bobby Don," said Pidgeon. "But Lloyd Cutler has security people five deep around him. Seems like he has a lot of enemies. If the Poes are after him, they won't get a shot at him. They get even close, they'll be seen and then arrested, if they're not killed first."

Du Pré followed her back into the study.

"How bad you think this is?" said Du Pré.

Pidgeon looked grim.

"Harvey says we really have to find them," she said.

Du Pré nodded.

"I didn't think we wanted to mention the rifle just yet, though," said Pidgeon.

"It is a lot of gun," said Du Pré.

"I know," said Pidgeon, "I know."

Du Pré went back to the kitchen.

"Pret' bad," said Madelaine.

Du Pré nodded.

They went out on to the deck. The day was beautiful, but it would be hot by afternoon.

"You got to find Poe and his cousin, Du Pré," said Madelaine.

"Up there, the mountains, there I know what to do," said Du Pré.

"You figure things out before," said Madelaine. "You figure this out."

Du Pré nodded.

He sat staring off at the great land.

· Chapter 27 ·

DU PRÉ FLIPPED OPEN his wallet. The police officer behind the Sheriff Department's bulletproof screen looked at his driver's license, his sheriff's deputy ID, and his badge. "Too-sant Mon-tana," the officer said.

Du Pré closed his wallet.

"You packing?" said the officer.

Du Pré shook his head.

"Empty your change and keys in here," said the officer, sliding out a plastic tray.

Du Pré did.

He walked through a metal detector, and then a buzzer sounded and he went into the hallway. The door slid back into the wall. Harvey Wallace was standing there. He nodded to Du Pré.

"Thanks for coming," he said.

"How's it going?" said Du Pré.

"Bobby Don is a cool customer," said Harvey. "He has a lawyer, which he insisted on, and he's going to walk out of here very shortly."

Du Pré followed Harvey down a brightly lit corridor and into a side room that had a big window in one wall, where the one-way mirror was set.

Bobby Don Poe was seated at a table; a man in a three-piece suit sat next to him. Two men in sport coats, men with thick necks and arms that strained the cloth, sat across from them.

"We still don't get it, Bobby," said one of the men. "Why are you here in Kansas?"

Bobby Don Poe looked at the man. "I don't get why I'm *here*," he said, and looked around the room.

"My client has cooperated," said the attorney. "You claim that he stole a nine-millimeter pistol. He didn't have it. You haven't any evidence that he did. You have held him here longer than the law allows. You keep asking the same questions, which don't have anything to do with a nine-millimeter pistol or anything else that might be called criminal. He could sue you for false arrest."

"Where's Hoyt?" said the other man.

"I've been tellin' you, Hoyt wanted a ride to Denver," said Bobby Don, "and I dropped him off at the bus station."

"Where was he going?" said the man.

"I don't know," said Bobby Don.

"Did he have the pistol?" said the man.

"What pistol," said Bobby Don, "are you talkin' of here?"

The men looked at each other.

"No one at the bus station saw Hoyt," said the man.

"I wasn't in the bus station," said Bobby Don, "so I can't tell you if they saw Hoyt or not."

The men looked at each other.

"Give us a minute," said one man, and he and the other got up and went out of the room.

Harvey laughed, quietly.

"They aren't getting much," he said.

Du Pré nodded.

The two men came into the room where Du Pré and Harvey were. One of them spread his hands.

"Not much of anything," he said.

"Of course," said the other, "we could arrest him under the Patriot Act and send him someplace we never even heard of . . ."

Harvey looked at them. "I assume you're joking, since Poe there is an American citizen and a decorated war hero and there would be a lot of questions."

The men nodded. "Bad joke," said one.

"What was in the truck?" said Harvey.

"A lot of crap: dog hair, a couple crushed beer cans about ten years old, a bag fulla dirty laundry, a lug wrench. Spare belt. A couple old bills," said one man.

"Nothin' and nada," said the other.

"Let him go," said Harvey.

The men both nodded.

"And stick on him like fucking stink on shit," said Harvey. "He takes a piss I want to know it."

"OK," said one of the men. "But this guy is just going to motorvate on home to his trailer, crack a beer, and watch the stock car races."

"You think?" said Harvey.

"You look at his service record?" said the man. "He got grabbed by some thugs in Iraq. They asked him this and that as only they can for two days and then our guys found him and them. Moment the stun grenade came in our guy there shouts, so his eardrums don't go, and when the guys come through the door, Bobby Don has managed to kick one of his friends in the nuts so hard guy nearly died. He told *them* nothing. Why would we think he'll give *us* anything?"

"We can follow him," said the man, "but he's cool. He won't so much as fart, so we could bust him for shooting at us."

"Do it anyway," said Harvey.

"It's pointless," said the man. "He's done his bit and now he cuts out. He's burned. He isn't gonna do dick."

Harvey nodded. "But it's possible he could be a target now, a little warning to his cousin."

"Well, we can watch for that, I guess," said the man. "Now, one piece of good news I was saving for last, we did get a Temple operative on the restaurant's security camera."

Harvey looked at him.

"But she's doing about what Bobby Don's been doing," said the man, "and she has a batch of evidence that says she was never anywhere near Spokane."

"Good evidence?" said Harvey.

"Good enough," said the man. "Lots of people. Lots of paper. Receipts. You know."

Du Pré looked at Harvey.

"She was at home," said the man, "the whole time."

Harvey sighed.

"At least we know we're in Kansas," said Harvey.

"Yup," said the man. "Now if we could just find Dorothy. Or Toto."

Harvey nodded.

The men went back into the room and told Bobby Don he could go.

Chapter 28

"I HAD SOME vacation time," said Harvey, "so I thought I would use it."

Du Pré looked at him.

"All right," said Harvey, "it isn't a vacation."

"La Salle," said Du Pré, "he calls, will we help, we help, now here we are, in Kansas."

"Which is between Montana and Texas, home of both Lloyd Cutler and Hoyt Poe," said Harvey. "My question still is, what is Hoyt planning to do?"

Du Pré shrugged.

"This bunch in Washington," said Harvey, "wipes their ass with the Bill of Rights. Poe does something, you could go down as an accessory."

Du Pré nodded. "But," he said, "that will not happen, because you will not let it happen. La Salle. Pidgeon. Bart. Foote."

"The guy sure has plenty of reasons to want to kill someone," said Harvey. "We just need to know who, exactly, he is planning to kill."

"I do not know," said Du Pré. They were sitting in a black Suburban in the lot by the sheriff's offices.

"Cutler's in Dallas," said Harvey.

Du Pré nodded.

"So," Harvey said, "if Hoyt decided to go to Dallas, then he's there now, if he had something to drive that would not attract attention."

"Yes," said Du Pré, "and if he is still in Denver, he could just be waiting."

Bobby Don Poe came out into the parking lot. He looked round for his pickup truck, spotted it, went over to it, lifted the hood.

"Go and talk to him," said Harvey.

Du Pré got out of the Suburban. He walked over to Bobby Don, who was peering into the engine compartment. He nodded, took folding pliers from a holster on his belt, reached inside. He clipped a wire. He reached in again and he felt for something. His fingers moved. He grunted. Then he went in with the pliers again.

He pulled out a blackened widget with four wires, two coming from each end. He set it down on the blacktop.

"That's one," he said.

Du Pré bent over, looked at it. "What is it?"

"Well, Du Pré," said Bobby Don, "it could be a radio signaller so these assholes think they know where I am, or it maybe could be a windshield wiper motor, or it could be a part on this fucking antique I don't know about and if I try to start it, it won't go. Take your pick." Bobby Don crawled under the truck.

"What now?" said Du Pré.

"Ah," said Bobby Don, "I wondered whether Kansas's Finest added something to my undercarriage. Looks like they didn't fuck around too much with this old piece of shit. But then, I asked them nicely to be careful when I was so rudely interrupted by six Highway Patrol cars and a fucking helicopterful of SWAT guys. I tell ya, Du Pré, it's gettin' so a man can't drive down the interstate without the goddamned government interferin'.'" Bobby Don slid out from under the truck.

"Now," he said, "maybe I want to start up old Myrtle here and go on home to my life in my little town . . ." Bobby Don stood up. "But on the other hand, I'm no expert in these things. Maybe I start up old Myrtle and find myself gone home to Jesus. Hoyt tells me he has a very high regard for you, Du Pré," said Bobby Don. "He said you were a good man and he trusted you."

Du Pré looked at the man, who looked back unblinking. "I don't want Hoyt dead," said Du Pré.

Bobby Don nodded.

"I don't want it either," said Bobby Don. "Do you suppose there is a place where we can go and talk without I have to wonder if I am making a hit record someplace?"

Du Pré pointed to the Suburban.

"If you say so," said Bobby Don.

They walked to it. They got in, Du Pré in front, Bobby Don in the back.

"Harvey Wallace," said Harvey, leaning over the seat. "FBI."

Bobby Don looked at Wallace. "Who are your people?" he said.

"Blackfeet," said Harvey.

"You're a long way from home," said Bobby Don. "Cherokee and Kiowa is mine." He pulled one of his long earlobes.

"So?" said Harvey.

"So I ain't eaten since I was picked up," said Bobby Don. "Whyn't we just head down this road a bit. There's a roadhouse there I eat at time to time, we can have some barbecue and a beer maybe."

Harvey started the engine, drove off.

He picked up his lapel and he said something into the microphone in it, took the earpiece out of his ear, and the sending unit out of his coat pocket.

He put all of the gear in a small box on the seat.

Bobby Don whistled, soft and low. The "Marines Hymn."

Harvey took the highway south, got up to speed.

They went about twenty miles and saw a low red building on the right, one with a few pickup trucks parked in front of it. Harvey pulled in.

"Owner don't like guns," said Bobby Don. "He can smell them. So leave it here."

Harvey took his SIG Sauer out of the holster and he put it on the floor of the cab.

He locked the Suburban up.

They went in.

The place was dark and it smelled wonderful, spiced pork and beer and old smoke and lemons.

The biggest man Du Pré had ever seen was behind the bar. He was so massive Du Pré felt puny. He wore a black turtleneck shirt and a leather vest, and rings on his fingers.

"Bo-Dine," said Bobby Don, "we would like some B-Q and brews."

Bodine looked at Du Pré for a long moment, then at Harvey.

"I don't want no trouble," said Bodine, looking at Harvey.

Harvey spread his hands.

"I mean I *really* don't want no trouble," said Bodine. He took a shotgun from underneath the bar. It had no stock, just a handgrip, and it had a magazine as long as the barrel.

"No trouble," said Harvey.

Bodine nodded. He drew beers, he shouted to the cook.

Bobby Don went to a table, sat.

Country music on the jukebox, bikers and cowboys at the bar.

"Now," said Bobby Don, "why are you-all tryin' to get me killed?"

"We aren't," said Harvey.

· Chapter 29 ·

BOBBY DON LIFTED HIS beer.

Du Pré looked at his fingers. The nails were odd, scar tissue at the bases, fingertips pitted.

. . . they were torn out . . . Du Pré thought.

A couple of the bikers looked at Harvey in his suit, measuring.

Bodine said something to them and they quit looking.

"What made you think there were explosives in your truck?" said Harvey.

Bobby Don looked at Harvey. "Because," said Bobby Don, "since you guys picked me up, I am a dead man one way or another. I knew I'd probably get picked up, you see, and when I did, somebody'd call somebody, 'cause they're after Hoyt. And now they're likely after me."

"If you can help us," said Harvey, "I can get you protection."

"Yeah," said Bobby Don, "like you pro-tected Sandy and little Faith Helen. Sure you can."

His laugh had a bitter twist.

"When I was checkin' on m' truck," said Bobby Don, "curtain in an office in the sheriff's building moved just a little. You got no idea how long these people's arm is. Somebody there was watchin', and maybe somebody there knows something about my truck. And maybe somebody was wishing I was dumb enough to get in pore ol' Myrtle and turn her on. Hope nobody back there was that dumb, either . . ."

Harvey nodded.

"So you think you can keep them from killin' me, Mister FBI, and let us say you can. But how long you going to do that? You quit on Hoyt and Sandy and the little girl," said Bobby Don. "You quit because pore Sandy never did have enough brains to fill a taco and she kept bustin' the rules. You bust the rules, you get stuck on a fencepost fer target practice . . ."

"It wasn't us," said Harvey.

"Not yer dee-partment," said Bobby Don. "Hoyt and Sandy and Faith Helen was supposed to be guarded by military security people. On account of Hoyt testifyin' about them animals tortured and murdered them Afghans. Hoyt was a good soldier and a good man and he done the right thing, and men get killed for that every day. Specially this war. So they use Hoyt, and then they dump him. Put him on a regular flight out of Washington to Spokane. They think 'cause it's a quick change it'll work. Only it don't work . . ."

"No," said Harvey. "It didn't."

"You done tried," said Bobby Don. "But I'll try to help you now because it's the right thing to do, not because you can protect me. Hoyt tol' me he saw somethin' at the restaurant, but Sandy was chewin' on his ear and he was so glad to see her and Faith Helen that he didn't think more about it then . . ."

"Jesus," said Du Pré.

"He wasn't mad at you, Du Pré," said Bobby Don. "He trusted you and he tol' me that. He concluded it was his fault for not paying more attention, though it didn't look like much at the time. Things kinda swell up later, when you know all of it . . ."

"Do you think this is all Temple's doing?" said Harvey.

"All Temple?" said Bobby Don. "Shit, man, you got these people in your own outfit, the regular po-lice, the military, all over the place. Temple is, you might say, just the easy-to-recognize ones, got all the toys. When I was mustered out, one of them come round, asked if I loved Jesus. Invited me to a li'l meetin' where they all loved Jesus together. His picture was right there on the wall next to Adolf Hitler's, another great admirer of Jesus. I took one look and said, no thank you, an' a feller sez 'yew sure?' and I said I was. He tol' me I ever mentioned this love-in fer Jesus I would be dead . . ."

"Christ," said Harvey.

"It gets a lot better," said Bobby Don. "When Hoyt sent the pictures to all the commanders—he wasn't dumb enough to send 'em to just one—he also sent them to a few journalists. Hoyt ain't the smartest man on dirt, but he was bright enough to see what he had to do. When I'm gettin' repaired at Walter Reed, I am in a ward, seven other guys. I get moved to a private room. Private rooms is for officers and not many of them. I am in there, this nurse got a pair of tits'd lift a stone man's pecker comes in, gives me a hand job, and asks if Hoyt's m' cousin. I don't say nothin' and so she concludes I am not gonna be helpful and away she goes . . ."

Harvey stopped chewing his barbecue.

"So it ain't just Temple," said Bobby Don. "When I get patched up enough so I can stagger, and I'm in good enough shape to go back, I want to, and I don't want to. I done my bit. I also think if I did go back, I'dda had to worry about more'n gettin' blowed up or mowed down by our Mideastern brothers. Now I make Temple and the rest nervous. So I take my walkin' papers, I am at a bar at the airport, waitin' to fly home, same pair of tits comes up and sticks her tongue in m' ear and sticks a nice thick envelope in m' carry-on bag. She says there's a lot of money in there and I can spend some of it with her if I like, long as I am quiet, and don't harm the work of the Lord . . ."

Harvey looked at Bobby Don.

"I opened the envelope," said Bobby Don. "Thirty thousand dollars and a note said there was more where that came from. I had half a thought of droppin' the envelope on the floor, and then I thought I might not make it home alive if I did that. If I kept it, well, they'd pray and hope I would come in."

Du Pré nodded.

Bobby Don finished the last of his barbecue. He finished his beer, picked up all three schooners, went to the bar. Bodine drew three more.

Bobby Don came back.

"There's a whole bunch of little towns down there to Texas," said Bobby Don, "phone book is about a half-inch thick fer all of them and half of that is Poes. You know our sort of people. We're the ones grow up and maybe get through high school, marry somebody we knowed since diapers was on us, have kids as fast as they kin fall down the well. And we been soldiers all along. Remember John Bell Hood? Confederate general. Dumb son of a bitch. He would attack anything. Lost an arm and a leg and it didn't slow him down. Us Poes was there, John Bell Hood's Texans, we got Poe bones on every battlefield ol' John Bell fought on. We done that war, and every war since. You got a war to fight, America does, and a whole passel of Poes shows up the next day. We ain't the questionin' sort of folks. We watch NASCAR and we work, the chicken plant or the feed plant, we go to church twice Sundays. We're dumber than Texas dirt and common as pig tracks but we make good soldiers, we just say 'yes, sir!' and off we go . . ."

Du Pré nodded.

"So America gets attacked and me and Hoyt joins up, like the good Poes we is. We ain't educated but we sure are always happy to do what we kin fer our country. So Hoyt and me go through our training, and we are real good at it and we get our little promotions and our photographs in our uniforms, and then we get to go and invade Afghanistan, stop them from attackin' us here in America. 'Cept we picked the wrong place. Country is fulla soldiers who could do us the kind of harm they been doin' since Alexander the Great invaded and he lost two divisions to 'em. Didn't have much to do with terrorism over there, but it had a lot to do with oil. Oh, we listened to the lies, but all soldiers get pretty good at tellin' lies from truth, even if we don't say much . . ."

Harvey was looking down into his beer.

"So," said Bobby Don, "there is me and Hoyt, growed to the right size for soldiers, and off we go. We growed up goin' to church, recitin' the Pledge of Allegiance, learnin' the Gettysburg Address, even if Lincoln was a damn Yankee. I make no claim to bein' all that smart, and things had fell a little different, why, Hoyt and me mighta liked Temple just fine. Weren't for Granny Dulcie Poe we might have . . ."

Harvey and Du Pré looked at him.

"Granny Dulcie was one of them people so good and so tough they make everybody around them better," said Bobby Don. "We had a mean preacher one time, used to yell about death and hellfire and how the Lord was a mean bastard. Granny Dulcie run him right out of the church, she had this big ol' snapping turtle in her hand, swinging it at him. She taught us a different Gospel. Hoyt and me was five or six, but what she taught us stuck. Granny Dulcie was somethin' . . ."

Harvey nodded.

"Me and Hoyt, we're in our current pickle 'cause of her," said Bobby Don. "She's been dead a long time but I would hate like hell to disappoint her in any way."

"BD!" yelled Bodine.

The huge man pointed to the screen on the TV.

There was a picture of Hoyt Poe, taken a while back, and he looked very young.

Another in his Marine Corps dress uniform, looking tough.

"This man is wanted, in a matter of national security,"

said the newscaster's voice. "If you have any information on Hoyt Poe, please call the number on your screen."

And then it was time for some blond woman to bubble about laundry soap.

· Chapter 30 ·

DU PRÉ AND HARVEY and Bobby Don walked out of the roadhouse to the black Suburban. A biker was sitting on his Harley next to it. He nodded to Bobby Don.

"Thanks," said Harvey. He and the biker shook hands.

"I dropped Hoyt off in Denver like he asked," said Bobby Don, "and more'n that I do not know. Felt I needed to do what he asked. He said nothing, nothing at all 'bout what he thought he would do. And I don't want to guess what he has a mind to . . ."

"He had Du Pré's sniper rifle," said Harvey.

"That's true," said Bobby Don, "but he wouldn't say how he planned to use it."

Harvey nodded. "You're smart enough to know whatever he planned was a bad idea," he said.

"No," said Bobby Don, "Poes been fightin' in all those wars and now this one, too, and I had a couple great-uncles said what might be the Poe motto was, 'We broke our ass for nothin.' We been lied to by so many people for so long and Hoyt just might be the Poe who finally had enough of the lies . . ."

"What are you going to do now?" said Harvey.

Bobby Don laughed.

"Try'n get home," he said. "A few of my Poe cousins are headed up t' git me. I trust Poes, least the ones I drunk beer with, ones have little kids call me 'uncle.' But not much of anybody else. They will be here shortly. I'm sorry I can't help you more'n I have, you understand. But I done my service. I give up m' fingernails fer the flag. I used to look at that flag and m' heart would swell up. I still look at it, but seems to be some strips of cloth sewed together, handy to spread over a pile of lies. I still got thirty-one pieces of shrapnel in me. I get a disability check. I got a medal. I killed a lot of people in Afghanistan with whom I had no quarrel. I regret that, like I regret bein' lied to. Pretty bad, you get lied to and go kill people and find out later, you shouldn't have. But we broke our ass for nothin' one more time. I kin go to the little grave-yard, go after dark, to home there, take a bottle of whiskey, set and tell Uncle Tuck and Uncle Gid 'Now I know what you meant. . . we broke our ass for nothing.'"

"I'm sorry," said Harvey.

"It's all right," said Bobby Don. "I know I'm probably a dead man and Hoyt for sure is a dead man. It's that kinda time now, here, you know, but there is just one thing I would ask of you two fellers . . ."

Du Pré and Harvey looked at Bobby Don.

He grinned.

"Just don't forget us. Don't forget me and Hoyt and all them Poes you never met. That's all. Just don't forget us. We done our best for you and we are prolly gonna get killed for doin' it," said Bobby Don. "It hadn't been fer Granny Dulcie, me and Hoyt mighta lived long lives, but she wouldn'ta wanted those lives for us. So blame Granny Dulcie for what happens to us two but you don't forget us, you hear . . . ?"

Harvey and Du Pré got in the black Suburban and Harvey paused before starting the engine and he and Du Pré looked at each other when it caught, relieved, and then they laughed.

"I thought maybe . . ." said Harvey.

"Me too," said Du Pré.

Harvey drove back north, through the town, past the sheriff's offices and Bobby Don Poe's abandoned pickup.

"Myrtle," said Harvey. "That's what he called her."

Du Pré rolled a smoke.

"You can't smoke in government vehicles," said Harvey. "Now roll one for me."

They went north, stopped for gas, got to the interstate.

They passed a strange building, set a half mile or so from the highway.

"Prison," said Harvey, "it's a growth industry."

"Why am I here?" said Du Pré.

"Du Pré," said Harvey, "I have two choices. I can leave this for the powers that be and let them do what they do and the hell with Hoyt Poe. Or I can try to figure out what Hoyt is going to do and where and try to save him from making the mistake of his life. I hope the two of us together can find him. He didn't deserve any of this, and I don't want him dead if we can manage to avoid that . . ."

Du Pré nodded.

"So," said Harvey, flicking his cigarette butt out the window, "what do you think he is going to do?"

Du Pré laughed.

"Bobby Don told us," said Du Pré.

"What the fuck," said Harvey, "do you mean?"

Du Pré fished a bottle of whiskey out of his bag and he had some and he offered the bottle to Harvey, who shook his head.

"He is not going to Texas," said Du Pré. "They knew Bobby Don would be picked up, knew probably there would be a manhunt, TV, the whole mess. They planned for that. So Hoyt, he has my rifle, he has my Glock, he is well trained. They try to make Texas look like where he's heading, but he's after one of the liars, he'll hunt him where we don't expect."

Harvey thought. "It's got to be Cutler," he said. "He's going after Cutler, but not in Texas."

"Hoyt left Montana with Bobby Don," said Du Pré. "Bobby Don did not lie to us. Hoyt got out in Denver."

"So we'd start turning Denver upside down?" said Harvey.

"And Bobby Don had a lot of money," said Du Pré. "So now Hoyt has a lot of money, buy a pickup, maybe, and start hunting . . ."

"OK, what do we know about Cutler when he's not in Texas," said Harvey. "I've heard he has a thing for fishing . . . like at a place in Montana? It's where plenty of rich Texans go."

Du Pré nodded.

"We go back to Montana, try our luck," said Du Pré. "Hoyt is maybe hunting there. What snipers are taught to do, to hunt."

"I have to take this Suburban back," said Harvey.

"We can fly," said Du Pré.

"And Pidgeon can check on where Cutler goes to fish," said Harvey.

Du Pré looked at him. "I think we will find them," he said.

"I had better call La Salle," said Harvey.

"*Non*," said Du Pré.

"What?" said Harvey.

Du Pré shook his head.

"Jack La Salle is not a part of this," said Harvey. "You know that."

"No," said Du Pré, "he is not."

"But there are others around him . . ." said Harvey.

"We can see if he wants to come and fish," said Du Pré.

· **Chapter 31** ·

THE LITTLE PLANE appeared in the east, a gleam of silver, a flash, then gone, then a gleam again.

It got closer, began to lose altitude.

Du Pré and Harvey waited by the small plane hangars, until the plane came in and the wheels touched down and it slowed and turned.

The plane headed for them, got to about fifty feet away, and the pilot cut the engine. The propeller whirled and slowed and stopped.

Jack La Salle got out.

An attendant on a tractor pulling a small tank came up beside the plane and began to refuel it.

La Salle nodded to Du Pré and Harvey.

"Bring your fishing pole?" said Harvey.

"Yes," said La Salle, "and it is called a fly rod."

They walked to the little plane, just big enough for three people, if the third one could crumple up enough to fit in the backseat, which was usually used as a luggage bay.

Du Pré folded himself in.

"I could get back there," said Harvey.

"*Non*," said Du Pré, "when we are pursued by a fighter jet we will throw you out, distract them."

"Oh," said Harvey.

He and La Salle got in, La Salle spoke to the tower, then he taxied the plane to the runway and he waited.

A passenger jet boomed out of the sky and shrieked and slowed on the long runway.

La Salle increased his engine speed. The plane trembled. He increased it more.

"Too much weight," Du Pré shouted close to Harvey's ear. "We will get airborne and then crash."

"Fuck you," said Harvey.

La Salle released the brakes and the plane moved forward. It picked up speed quickly, but then seemed to run a long way before it lifted very slowly off the pavement.

La Salle headed east, slowly climbing. It took fifteen minutes to get enough altitude to level out.

"Well," said La Salle, "we were a few pounds over the suggested payload. Air is thinner up this high, so takeoff was slower. I must write a nice note to the builder."

"What is the payload supposed to be?" said Harvey.

"Me and Du Pré and some baggage," said La Salle. "How much do you weigh?"

"Two-twenty," said Harvey.

"A very nice note to the manufacturer," said La Salle.

The earth was far below.

Du Pré could see the plane's shadow cross the land under them.

"So," said La Salle, "I take it we are of a mind. We would like to find Hoyt before he wrecks what little he has left of his life."

"Yes," said Harvey, "if he is really here. If he isn't on his way to somewhere in Texas."

La Salle nodded.

"That poor bastard," said La Salle. "His country has not done well by him."

"The country is fine," said Harvey. "It's those bastards got him into that stupid mess that aren't."

"I agree," said La Salle, "and I misspoke."

"I want to help the guy," said Harvey. "Of course, if I had knowledge of a crime and I did not report it . . ."

"You'd be canned," said La Salle.

"No crime," said Du Pré.

Harvey looked at him.

"I don't sign a complaint for theft, my rifle," said Du Pré, "there is no crime."

"No," said Harvey, "but you just might get an accessory charge."

La Salle corrected his course.

"There are the Wolf Mountains," said La Salle, pointing.

A faint gray scribble behind the distant pale ocher plains.

Forty minutes later they were coming into the meadow. The windsock was limp and the sheep that grazed the runway grass were all in a paddock at the far end.

All but two. La Salle came in and the two sheep stood there, looking dumbly at the little plane.

Then they ambled slowly out of the way.

La Salle set the plane down.

It bounced.

It bounced a lot.

Du Pré hit his head on the ceiling.

Then the plane slowed and La Salle turned and taxied back toward the fence by the road.

Pidgeon was standing there, with one of the ranch Suburbans.

La Salle stopped the engine and Du Pré waited until Harvey had gotten out, groaning, and then he unfolded himself.

La Salle fished gear out of the fuselage: a small fishing bag, a rod tube, a carry-on bag, and a computer in a case. Du Pré got out the few things he and Harvey had brought.

A man in a cowboy hat driving an ATV came up the road. He opened a long gate and he drove in and he fastened a harness to the little plane and he began to tow it out to the road. La Salle helped him get the plane turned, and then the man went off, the plane moving along briskly behind him.

"This is the only place I ever flew into," said La Salle, "where the county road crew moves the trucks out of the building to make room for light aircraft."

"High winds tomorrow," said Pidgeon.

They all got in the Suburban.

Pidgeon drove out to the ranch. She drove very fast, fishtailing around turns as she blithely ignored physics and ditches.

She pulled up next to the main house.

Booger Tom was sitting on the steps, whittling something.

They all got out.

The old cowboy stood up. "La Salle," he said.

"Booger Tom," said La Salle, "you in on this?"

"Last I checked," said Booger Tom. "It was my country too."

"Oh, yes," said La Salle.

"That young feller," said Booger Tom, "sure don't deserve none of this."

"No," said La Salle.

They all went in.

Bart was cooking. It smelled wonderful, tomatoes and spices and searing meat. He served up spaghetti and sausages and meatballs, crusty bread and good red wine.

Madelaine came halfway through dinner. She got a plate and she served herself and she joined them at the big round table by the window that framed the distant Wolf Mountains.

"You find anything on Cutler's retreat?" said Harvey.

Pidgeon looked at him. "Nope," she said. "Nothing in Montana for Cutler, nothing for Temple Security, nothing for any of Cutler's other businesses."

Du Pré had some red wine.

"You try Wyoming?" said Harvey. "Jackson Hole?"

"Sure," said Pidgeon, "and I looked at all the other rich fuck ghettoes. Not a thing."

Harvey looked at Du Pré.

Du Pré shrugged.

"But Cutler's a cheap bastard," said Pidgeon. "Kinda guy always on his employees about little shit, you know . . ."

Harvey looked at Pidgeon, his eyes narrowing.

"So," said Pidgeon, "if Cutler comes up here to fly-fish, on account of him being such a gentleman, he rents a few rooms, maybe, in a lodge someplace. He's paranoid, so he needs accommodations for four, five bodyguards . . ."

"Pidgeon," said Harvey, "OK, we're stupid, we are just guys . . ."

"Yeah," said Pidgeon, "and don't expect mercy. Cutler's careful. He's cheap. He rents. Hard to follow. But actually, we care about Cutler only because he's the goat and we want the tiger, right?"

"Pidgeon," said Harvey. "Just tell us."

"So," said Pidgeon, "I thought I'd see if the tiger knew anybody in the fish biz."

Harvey put his head in his hands.

"It was right there in the emails on Sandy's computer," said Pidgeon.

"Hoyt's second cousin. Banner Vardaman."

· **Chapter 32** ·

"HARVEY IS SORRY to miss this," said Du Pré, "but might be just as well they call him back from vacation. Maybe keep the lid on there, Washington, long enough for us to find Poe here."

He cruised through the little town, past an abandoned state building and a forlorn school, now boarded up. There were three bars, a small grocery store, and six fishing shops, all having sand-blasted redwood signs with either trout flies or jumping fish on them. A lot across the street was packed with guide boats.

"What did they used to have here?" said La Salle.

"Cattle and sheep," said Du Pré. "Lots of sheep, it was good pasture in the mountains. Some wheat . . ."

"And now they have fly-fishing," said La Salle.

"Have to make all their money in sixty days," said Du Pré.

"I'm sorry," said La Salle.

"The buffalo are gone too," said Du Pré. He turned around and they went back to the town center and Du Pré parked the old cruiser.

"It's that one," said La Salle.

They got out and they went inside the shop. The walls were hung with packets of feathers, spools of thread, boxes of hooks in plastic bags, rods, rod cases, and a glass-fronted cabinet with a display of fishing reels.

There was no one in the place.

"Hello?" said La Salle.

"Be with you in a minute," said a deep voice, a soft drawl.

A man came out of the back of the store.

He was white-haired and his face carried old splotches of scar tissue on his forehead and left cheek.

"Good afternoon," said La Salle. "I believe I am addressing Staff Sergeant Vardaman?"

"Ree-tired," said Vardaman.

The door opened, two red-faced men came in. They were laughing.

"What flies are doing good?" said one.

Vardaman gestured to a small blackboard.

Bitch Creek, Elkhair Caddis, Madame X, Gold Ribbed Hare's Ear.

The dudes picked through the flies in the fly cabinet, an old mail rack converted and set at an angle. They brought their flies to the counter; Vardaman looked up.

"Eighty-four fifty," he said.

The man gave him a hundred-dollar bill. Vardaman made change.

He put the flies in a cheap plastic box.

"We'll bring 'em back, they don't work!" said the man.

He went out, with his friend, laughing.

"Hope you cocksuckers drown," said Vardaman, looking at the closed door. He turned back to La Salle.

"Now how may I help you fellers?" he said.

"We want to fish," said La Salle.

Vardaman smiled, his lips were crooked.

"Bullshit," he said. "If yer cops, get the fuck out of my store 'less you got a warrant . . ."

"We aren't cops," said La Salle. "I am General Jack La Salle, this is Lieutenant Du Pré . . ."

"That's real nice," said Vardaman, "now what are we gonna invade?"

"Where's Hoyt?" said La Salle.

"Down to the family farm, I would guess," said Vardaman. "It's that way 'bout fifteen hundred miles." He pointed southeast.

"We want to help him," said La Salle.

"Whatcha gonna do?" said Vardaman, "give him a fucking medal? I got four myself. Traded my face for 'em . . ."

"First Gulf War," said La Salle.

Vardaman nodded.

"One of them smart bombs went dumb," he said, "killed seven of my men and mangled the rest of us. I got off the easiest. Now why don't you just whistle the 'Star-Spangled Banner' on yer way out the door?"

"Hoyt was fucked," said La Salle. "I want the people who did that, goddamn it. I don't want him dead or in prison for the rest of his life."

Vardaman looked at La Salle.

"Like I said," he said. "You try the family farm. It's about big enough t' raise two hogs and chickens enough t' feed the family. Hoyt's likely down there, bathin' the hogs. On a good day, he'll treat himself to an ice cream cone, polish his medals, go to the cemetery, and look at where his wife and kid are."

"You want him dead too?" said La Salle. "He's out there with a fifty-caliber sniper rifle. I know who he wants to kill. I don't blame him for wanting to do it. But if he does it, then everything is destroyed for him. You understand?"

Vardaman looked at La Salle and Du Pré.

"You two assholes roll out the door," he said, "I got nothing to say to you . . ."

La Salle stalked over to the counter. "Soldier," he said, "don't disappoint me." He locked eyes with Vardaman.

"It will only help the people who hurt Hoyt," said Du Pré. "Make a martyr of Cutler and then they go on."

Vardaman came round the counter, went to the front door, locked it, put a sign in the window.

He nodded toward the back.

They followed him through a dusty green velvet curtain.

The back room was huge, and it held strange machinery, old castings painted black, with brass fittings and nameplates. The walls were filled with racks that held bamboo strips, a long workbench with an elaborate clamping system took up most of the center of the room. La Salle went to one of the machines.

"My God," he said. "Where did you find these?"

"After I got mustered out," said Vardaman, "I had to figure out what I was gonna do with the rest of my life. I wanted to do somethin' wasn't like anything I had done. Always kinda liked fly-fishing. Used to go up to Colorado with m' pa and fish; we wasn't a bit of good, but I liked it. So I looked round, found these machines in a warehouse in Houston. Part of an estate, lawyer took 'em in payment, sold 'em to me. Purest luck. Made in the 1880s, Hatch and Son, Birmingham, England. There ain't many of them left. There weren't many to begin with."

La Salle looked at a bamboo rod, clamped and drying on the bench.

He touched a long strip of cane.

"You kin pick it up," said Vardaman. "Got a hickey in it, some damn bug et it long time ago, too weak to use now."

La Salle picked up the strip, which flopped loose in his hands.

He looked at Du Pré.

"These machines taper the cane strips," said La Salle. "There just aren't many old-line rod makers left these days."

"Ain't that many idiots want to pay four grand for a fish pole," said Vardaman.

He went to a drawer, pulled out a bottle of whiskey, and he found three old jars, small ones, like jelly comes in.

He blew dust out of them. "Chinese used to put powdered bamboo in whiskey they give to assholes they wanted dead," said Vardaman. "I'm feelin' nice today so I done blew most of it out."

"Where is Hoyt?" said La Salle, over the top of his jelly jar.

"I tol' you," said Vardaman, "prolly to home, buryin' Sandy and little Faith Helen . . ."

"Christ," said La Salle.

Vardaman laughed. "I ain't lyin' to you," he said. "You looked up stuff on yer *com*-puter and come here on account of Hoyt's kin of mine. But I ain't seen him. He sent me a couple messages. How was I, what was I up to, how was the fishing."

"He hasn't seen you or you him?" said La Salle.

Vardaman shook his head.

"Temple Security," said La Salle. "You know about them?"

Vardaman looked at him.

"What about 'em?" he said.

La Salle looked at Du Pré, then at Vardaman. "Hoyt's after Lloyd Cutler," said La Salle. "I'm sure of that."

Vardaman nodded. He looked off, someplace far away.

"Wonderful world, ain't it," said Vardaman. "But the truth of the matter, General, is I got no idea where Hoyt is. You see, if Hoyt's about what you say he is, he would not get anyone else into trouble over it. He's what's called a *solus*. A man alone. Latin. I ain't bright enough to read novels so I read dictionaries, they ain't so hard to follow . . ."

La Salle nodded.

Vardaman sighed. "Cutler's comin'," he said. "Does every year. Rents the little lodge out to a ranch here went to bein' a fly-fishin' whorehouse . . ."

"OK," said La Salle.

Vardaman sighed. "All right, count me in," he said. "I'm family. It may not be much, General, but it might just be enough."

· **Chapter 33** ·

THEY WENT OUT the back door and around the corner of the building, and Vardaman led Du Pré and La Salle to the main street. He pointed south, to a saloon.

"I'm feelin' dry," said Vardaman.

An expensive SUV pulled up in front of them and the windows came down. "You Banner Vardaman?" said a fleshy man, his head sideways out the window.

"Yup," said Vardaman, "an' m' shop's closed for the day." He started walking.

Du Pré and La Salle followed.

The SUV backed up.

"I want to order some rods," said the man.

"You kin write me a letter," said Vardaman. "I said I'm closed today."

"Do you know who I am?" the man said, red-faced.

Vardaman stopped.

"Yer a farina-faced glob of rich puke from some stinking asshole of a city and that's enough to know," said Vardaman. "Now go fuck yerself. I wouldn't make a rod for you, you paid in gold . . ."

Vardaman walked on.

Du Pré and La Salle followed him into the saloon.

"Hi there, missy," said Vardaman to the pretty young woman behind the bar. "We'd like somethin' to drink . . ."

"Whiskey ditch," said La Salle, and Du Pré nodded.

"Make three," said Vardaman. "Say, honey, you got that leaded pool cue under the bar there? Maggie wanted me to see it, sez it has a split . . ."

The girl nodded, pulled out the pool cue. It was a little less than four feet long and had a metal ball at the thick end.

Vardaman waved to a small table by the wall and La Salle and Du Pré went to it and sat.

Vardaman lounged at the bar.

The door opened suddenly and two big men, heavily muscled and young, came in and they charged straight for Vardaman.

The man who had accosted Vardaman from the SUV was behind them.

Vardaman lunged forward, poking the first bodyguard in the gut with the thin end of the cue, and the man shrieked and fell, and then Vardaman whacked the other high on the chest. A bone snapped and the man stumbled back.

The older man behind them turned white, wheeled around, and fled. Vardaman looked at the bodyguard who was holding his broken collarbone. "Get him out of here," said Vardaman, nodding at the bodyguard puking his guts out on the floor, "and tell that fat fuck I see him here again I will speak to him rudely . . ."

The standing bodyguard helped the other to a crouch and they went on out the door.

"Hell of a salesman," said La Salle.

"I make good rods," said Vardaman. "I don't have to put up with bad manners . . ."

A rail-thin man in a tan uniform came in, blinked a moment after he took off his dark glasses.

He saw Vardaman.

"I got this complaint," said the sheriff, "a-saultin' two fellers."

"They jumped him," said the girl behind the bar, "the brutes."

The sheriff nodded.

"Well," he said, "that's different."

"I'm just an old crippled fly rod maker," said Vardaman, "harmless as an old dog."

"Guy's out there hollerin' about suin' everybody, includin' God," said the sheriff.

"Tell him I'll jes' sue him back," said Vardaman. "Billion-aires hate that, I hear."

The sheriff put on his dark glasses.

"Glad you got a witness," he said. "One guy's still pukin'. I expect they will find themselves outta the bodyguard business. So look, just don't *kill* anybody, Ban. I ask that as a personal favor. We got this little scam here, ripping off fishermen and it would not do, we had the locals killin' 'em."

Vardaman pulled up his right pant leg. He had a steel prosthesis.

"I'm just a pore old crippled rod maker," said Vardaman again, "harmless as a toothless old dog . . ."

"Ah, fuck you," said the sheriff, "just remember what I said." And he went back out the door.

"Thanks, angel," said Vardaman.

The young woman gave him a dazzling smile.

"Any time," she said.

"Christ," said Vardaman, "a feller can't even go get hisself a drink with two of his new best friends without some assholes screwin' it up. I tell ya, it is a hard and dangerous world out there . . ."

"So," said La Salle, "what do you suggest?"

Vardaman leaned over the table.

"I know the folks have the fly-fishing lodge," he said, "so I expect I should mosey on out there and find out what I can.

If Hoyt's goin' for Cutler, be nice to know just when Cutler is gonna be here . . ."

La Salle nodded.

"Then we can worry," said Vardaman. "That rifle got a range of a mile and a half accurate and three not so good . . ."

"Or it will go through an inch of armor plate at a half mile," said La Salle.

"Like it was designed to do," said Vardaman. "Where'd Hoyt get the damn thing anyway? They cost some money."

"He borrowed it from me," said Du Pré.

"Oh," said Vardaman.

"He forgot to leave a note," said Du Pré.

"Well," said Vardaman, "young folks these days."

They drank their ditches and the young woman brought three more.

"He's younger than we are and stronger," said Vardaman, "smarter, too, probably. He's been trained. He's been trained not to be overtrained too."

La Salle nodded.

Du Pré looked at him.

"Initiative," said La Salle. "Snipers are selected for intelligence and a willingness to think in all situations . . ."

"He isn't gonna do it by the book," said Vardaman, "on account he will figure folks tryin' to stop him will have read the book too."

"Cutler will come with bodyguards," said Du Pré.

"Yup," said Vardaman, "I hear he has shootin' contests and the winners get to be his bodyguards. Head guy is named Stoltz. Been with Cutler for a long time. Maybe even made some people disappear, no proof, of course."

"You seem to know a lot about this," said La Salle.

Vardaman looked at him. "How long you known about these people?" he said.

La Salle shrugged.

"They left me alone," said Vardaman, "but they got after a couple of my younger kin. One of them signed on. He ended up in burnt chunks hung off a bridge in Baghdad . . ."

La Salle nodded.

"Kid wanted out, he said, when he wrote home. It wasn't exactly what he'd been told. Said he thought he was going to provide security but it wasn't quite like that . . ." said Vardaman.

La Salle looked at Vardaman.

"So he writes home, nothing he says is very specific, next day he and three others was sent off to do somethin' or other. But they was given a map took them right into a part of Baghdad nobody goes to without a couple tanks and air cover . . ." said Vardaman.

La Salle looked grim.

"So," said Vardaman, "nothing to prove anything, you see, but it did stink."

"I'm sorry," said La Salle.

Vardaman shrugged.

"There was a few of 'em when I was in," he said. "You know, the kind preached the end of the world and Jesus is coming, soon as we kill all the A-rabs."

La Salle nodded.

"There's more'n a few now," said Vardaman.

La Salle nodded.

"You sure you want to stop Hoyt?" said Vardaman.

But he had a half smile when he said it.

· Chapter 34 ·

VARDAMAN STOOD UP, went to the bar, paid, left a tip for the young woman. He tipped his hat to her and he went toward the door.

Du Pré and La Salle followed.

"I was you," said Vardaman, "I wouldn't rent me a motel room. I would expect Cutler's crew to be paying you unwanted attention, myself. Ol' Cutler, there, likes to get ugly when he thinks he is in danger of havin' his head blowed off. Which he is . . ."

Du Pré nodded.

"So," said Vardaman, "you go on up that street there, and you will find a yeller house got a Land Rover out front. It is a Land Rover, I do guarantee it, but it is a bit worn here and there. Front door of the house is never locked. There's a big black Alsatian name of Harry inside there, who aspires to bein' tough. He will offer to eat you through the door glass. What you do is tell him to cut it out. Them three words. You yell them. And he will. There's two rooms the back there, off the kitchen. Beer in the fridge and whiskey in the cupboard over the toaster."

"We are much obliged," said La Salle.

"And I will go ask the feller who owns that goddamned fly-fishing bordello about this and that. He's a good sort, almost went bust in the beef business . . ." said Vardaman, stepping outside, "and his son joined the National Guard, and guess where he is . . ."

Du Pré and La Salle walked toward the cruiser, which was parked behind a battered old Volkswagen.

A late-model Cadillac roared up the street and it braked by Vardaman. A woman in a pinstriped suit got out. "You fucking bastard!" she yelled. "I had that guy ready to buy a property worth three mil and you fuck it up, you goddamned cocksucker!"

Vardaman looked at her. "Why, Lucille," he said, "it is always so lovely to see you . . ."

"You son of a bitch," she screamed, "he came over here to order some fly rods. And you treat him like shit. And you beat the crap out of his bodyguards! He was beside himself!"

"He didn't have any manners," said Vardaman.

The woman took a swing at Vardaman, and he ducked.

"Now, Lucille," he said, "you're overwrought."

"You fucker," she said, "I needed that commission."

"Ah, hell, Lucille," said Vardaman, "there'll just be another one of 'em along. And they never do like us natives anyway."

"Native? You Texas prick, you only been here . . ." she spluttered and choked.

"Eleven years," said Vardaman. "I know yer family's been here since 1881. Fine old Montana family. Usual story, yer great-grandma couldn't turn enough tricks to make it to the coast . . ."

"Goddamn son of a bitch," said Lucille.

"I had me a headache," said Vardaman. "Made me tetchy."

Lucille took a deep breath. "He went roaring out of here, screaming he was never gonna set foot in Montana again . . ."

"Really?" said Vardaman. "Shit, Lucille, you oughta love me for it, guy was an asshole . . ."

Lucille walked back to her Cadillac. She got in, slammed the door, drove off.

Vardaman held out his hands, palms up, and then he grinned. He got into a battered Volkswagen bug and started the tiny engine. He drove off.

Du Pré and La Salle got in the cruiser and they drove down the street Vardaman had pointed to.

A Land Rover so battered and rusted it looked ready to fall apart sat in front of a yellow house.

. . . Tires are very new though . . . Du Pré thought.

They walked up to the porch and a huge black dog appeared in the oval glass of the front door. He scrabbled at the glass and he barked and raged.

"Harry!" La Salle yelled. "CUT IT OUT!"

Harry dropped to all four paws. His tail began to wag.

La Salle opened the door and he went in. Harry sat, and La Salle said, "Good boy."

Du Pré patted the huge black head.

They walked into the kitchen. La Salle fished two beers out of the fridge. Du Pré looked around the room. It was clean and neat, though shabby and worn. Dishes sat in a rack by the sink. Bundles of silver sage hung from strings in the kitchen window.

Du Pré took his beer and he went out the back door. There was a big yard with a tall blue spruce tree toward the back, a high fence, a doghouse, and carefully tended flower beds, now full of poppies and delphiniums.

Harry came out to join him.

Du Pré sat down in an old wicker chair.

La Salle came out. He sat on the steps. "What do you think?" he said.

"We are lucky," said Du Pré.

"Is he lying?" said La Salle.

Du Pré shook his head.

"I mean, is he lying about Hoyt, that Hoyt hasn't contacted him?" said La Salle.

Du Pré shrugged.

"I don't think so," he said. "I think he hoped Hoyt wasn't coming here. But now he knows . . ."

"We aren't sure," said La Salle.

Du Pré rolled a smoke. "I am sure," he said.

La Salle nodded.

"Well," he said, "if Hoyt wants to kill Cutler, this is a good place. Cutler will be on the river, and that gives Hoyt a perfect opportunity to take his shot . . ."

Du Pré nodded. He lit his cigarette. Offered his pouch to La Salle, who took it.

"Haven't had one of these in a long time," said La Salle. He rolled a smoke, lumpily. He lit it.

"Christ," he said, coughing, "this is lousy tobacco."

Du Pré laughed.

"Good of Vardaman to put us up," said La Salle.

"He wants to know where we are," said Du Pré.

Harry fetched a big green ball and he held it in his mouth, looking hopefully at La Salle.

"All right," said La Salle, "give me that . . ."

He took the ball and he threw it. Harry raced to it, grabbed it, raced back.

"Bozo," said La Salle, throwing the ball again.

"There is something else," said Du Pré, "it bothers me."

La Salle looked at him.

Harry came back with the ball, sat waiting by La Salle.

"I don't know if Hoyt cares about getting away," said Du Pré. "He will be very hard to find and stop if he is like that . . ."

La Salle thought. "And Cutler may not be the only target," he said.

Du Pré nodded.

"Vardaman," said La Salle, "is one funny man." He threw the ball for Harry again. "So what are we going to do?" he said.

"Find out more about Cutler," said Du Pré.

La Salle nodded. "Maybe," he said, "I could stir the shit a little."

Du Pré looked at him.

"If Cutler isn't here," said La Salle, "Hoyt can't kill him."

Harry brought the ball, and La Salle tossed it.

Du Pré closed his eyes. . . . How have we come to this? . . . he thought.

Chapter 35

LUCILLE THE REAL estate lady stood in Vardaman's rod workshop, well dressed, well shod, and in no mood for bullshit.

"Vardaman," she said, "I have a client coming over here and if you fuck *this* up I will kill you. KILL YOU!"

Du Pré and La Salle looked at each other.

"Lucille," said Vardaman, holding a milled blank of cane in his hands, "yer standin' in the light."

"You hear me?" she said.

"I heard you, Lucille," said Vardaman. "Now why don't we just go and get drunk and screw?"

"I may have sunk low, Vardaman," said Lucille, "but not that low. Now, Lloyd Cutler is coming here to order a fly rod. He has the ability to pay for it. You make your living selling your very expensive fly rods. You are gonna sell one to him and you are not gonna insult him like you usually do everybody else."

"They love it," said Vardaman. "Like that journalist feller from that slick magazine come here and wanted to fish. Editor calls and tells me how good it would be fer m' business to see his ree-porter had a good time. Ree-porter called me 'crusty.' You remember?"

Lucille looked at him, eyes hard.

"I remember you took that poor bastard over to the Big Hole and gave him what you said was insect lotion that just happened to have sugar in it and he about died from blood loss, between those Big Hole mosquitoes and the no-see-ums, and every bite one of those little bastards give him got infected and now the reporter looks like he either had bad acne as a kid or he took a load of birdshot in the face . . ." said Lucille. "Now you listen. Cutler's business manager said he was interested in a big property and I got one I really want to sell him."

"Lucille," said Vardaman, "I still say let's go get drunk and screw."

"Fuck you, you goddamned TEXAN!" she snarled, and she turned and strode out of the shop.

The front door slammed.

"I oughta sue her fer castin' ass-persions on Texans," said Vardaman. "These Montanans *hate* Texans. I never seen anything like it. It violates my civil rights, it does . . ."

Du Pré laughed.

"See you later," said La Salle. "Have a good time."

"Yeah," said Vardaman. "I doubt Hoyt will think to use me fer bait, but it would be a good idea you sorta kept an eye out there while Cutler is here at the shop. Us not knowin' where Hoyt is, exactly, and all . . ."

"He would have no way of knowing that Cutler was coming to your shop," said La Salle.

"We don't know what he knows," said Vardaman.

"True," said La Salle.

He and Du Pré went out to the cruiser parked across the street. They got in.

La Salle shook his head.

Du Pré looked at him.

"Banner Vardaman," said La Salle. "I looked at his records. He wants us to believe he's just a bulk-run redneck. But his IQ is around one-sixty, and when he decided to go into the rod business, he found and bought the machinery, which had been in a warehouse for thirty years, and he read what he could find on making rods, and he moved here and in three months he was making cane rods so well he had more orders than he had time to fill them."

Du Pré nodded.

"So what now?" said La Salle.

"Nothing much to do, right now," said Du Pré.

La Salle nodded. "Then let's get some lunch," he said, pointing to the restaurant across the street.

They went in and took the table by the front window.

They ate and had just finished when three black Suburbans with dark windows pulled up in front of Vardaman's shop.

A man got out and he looked around, and then three others got out of the rear vehicle. Another got out of the center vehicle and he went inside and then when he came back, two more people got out.

Lloyd Cutler was dressed in stylish fishing clothes: a light blue shirt with a lot of pockets and baggy tan pants and wading shoes.

He went into the shop with one of his bodyguards.

The others stood outside, looking up and down the street. They all wore plain black suits and white shirts with black ties.

La Salle put a twenty and a ten on the table and he and Du Pré headed toward the door.

They saw the bodyguard who was standing closest to the front door to the shop suddenly whirl around and run through the door.

Du Pré and La Salle ran across the street.

A police car with lights flashing screeched to a halt in front of the shop and the sheriff got out, yelling at the other bodyguards.

Two more sheriff's department cars roared up, stopped, deputies got out, all carrying shotguns in their hands.

A Highway Patrol car arrived, and the patrolman got out.
The sheriff was standing in Vardaman's doorway, gun in
his hand.

La Salle and Du Pré walked over to the door and paused
as the sheriff moved inside.

"Back off," said a deputy, who now stood in the open
doorway. An ambulance roared up and two medics got out,
grabbed their kits, and ran inside.

La Salle opened his wallet. He shoved the wallet near the
deputy's eyes. "Out of my way, mister," he said.

. . . General La Salle . . . thought Du Pré.

La Salle beckoned to Du Pré and they went in. A bodyguard sprawled inside the doorway and a man lay facedown
at the back of the shop. Cutler.

A thin trickle of blood ran over the linoleum by his
head.

The air smelled of cordite.

One of the medics had his finger on Cutler's throat. He
shook his head.

The other bodyguard was slumped against a workbench,
and he had a small hole just above his eyes in the center of
his forehead.

The sheriff and Vardaman were standing back by the cane
racks. "I dunno what it was about," said Vardaman. "Cutler
went off and he pulled out that pistol there and his bodyguard went for his. I just grabbed my popgun there, it happened kinda fast . . ."

"Christ, Ban," said the sheriff.

"An' that other one come piling through the front door,"
said Vardaman, "had his gun out, so I squeezed off a shot
while I was duckin' down . . ."

"What the hell are you doing here?" said the sheriff, seeing
La Salle and Du Pré for the first time.

"This should explain it," said La Salle, flipping open his
wallet.

The sheriff looked at the cards. "Oh, my my," he said, "the feds are gonna help."

"You want the state crime lab boys?" said the Highway Patrolman.

"You bet I do," said the sheriff.

"I'll tell them just what I told you, Bud," said Vardaman. "I was talkin' to Cutler and he was lookin' at some pictures of rods there, on the computer, and next thing I know he has that gun in his hand."

"And you just happened to have yours handy," said the sheriff.

"It's a dangerous world, Bud," said Vardaman, "an' I got post-traumatic stress syndrome. It's why I moved here for the peace and quiet . . ."

The medics were standing now. "Nothing we can do here," they said. "What do you want?"

"Just leave them for the crime scene crew," said the sheriff.

"I'm feelin' the need to get out of here," said Vardaman, "the stress is awful."

"Everybody out," said the sheriff. "Close it up until the staties come and do their thing."

He and Vardaman and La Salle and Du Pré went out the front door.

The bodyguards were talking among themselves.

"I am going to want to talk to you all," said the sheriff. "So you let my deputy over there know where we can find you. And you just leave them Suburbans right where they sit."

"You gonna arrest me, Bud?" said Vardaman.

The sheriff looked at him.

"Damn right," he said. "Protective custody. Lucille is gonna tear out your liver and eat it when she hears about this . . ."

The driver's door in the third Suburban opened and a woman got out. She had short blond hair and she wore wrap-around sunglasses and a black jumpsuit with a lot of pockets.

Du Pré looked at her. She ignored him. She said something into a phone and walked away.

"I know her," Du Pré whispered to La Salle. "She is on the restaurant tape, before they kill Hoyt's wife and daughter."

La Salle just shook his head.

· Chapter 36 ·

PIDGEON CAME OUT of the county building that stood one street over from Vardaman's fly shop. She leaned against one of the pillars by the front door and she lit a cigarette. She rubbed her eyes with her fingers.

Du Pré was lounging against the hood of his old cruiser.

He waved.

Pidgeon came down the steps and across the parking lot.

"I've left La Salle in with Vardaman," she said. "Such fun and more on the way. Harvey was beside himself. He was back in his office for the first time in a month and hoo-boy . . ."

It was just getting dark. The day had been hot and now it was cool.

Pidgeon was wearing a sleeveless blouse and slacks and a leather belt with a turquoise-and-silver buckle the size of a hamburger bun.

"The state police technicians are still going over the shop," she said, "and they'll be at it for a good while longer. But so far, there's nothing to dispute Vardaman's account of what happened. It's just that we know that son of a bitch set Cutler and his boys up. He set us all up . . ."

Du Pré nodded.

"So Cutler comes here, maybe to buy some fly-fishing property," said Pidgeon, "but for sure to buy one of Vardaman's big-status fly rods. What we don't know is what would have set Cutler off. Vardaman said Cutler fired once, the first shot. Slug we dug out of the wall matches Cutler's nine-millimeter. Vardaman is using a twenty-two mag with hollow points. He taps Cutler. Cutler's bodyguard draws his pistol but Vardaman puts one in him and then the bodyguard shoots once into the ceiling, a convulsive reaction. Two down. Fifteen seconds later the guard by the door gets one through the right eye into the brain. Whole business, start to finish, less than twenty seconds."

"Good shooting," said Du Pré.

"Yeah," said Pidgeon, "and then Vardaman hits his alarm system, a good one, and it happens that the locals are all in town at that moment and they all hear the address. They all know it's Vardaman's place, and"—she snapped her fingers— "there they are. Now, I don't know for sure what would have happened if they hadn't come, but come they did, and now we have Vardaman in this fine county building, drawling away about how upsetting it all is and how sad he feels for the families of the three men he just took down, who it seems were preparing to kill *him*. What I want to know is just how Vardaman managed to pull this off. How'd he start it?"

"He said he was showing Cutler pictures of fly rods, the computer," said Du Pré.

Pidgeon looked at him and laughed. "The techies looked at the computer for a long time," she said, "and all they saw were pictures of fly rods."

"He could have said something," said Du Pré. "Said something to Cutler that set him off."

"I did wonder about that," said Pidgeon.

"Vardaman knew Cutler was coming," said Du Pré. "He told us that and then he played us well. Hospitality. You come stay, my place, I will help."

"Uh-huh," said Pidgeon.

"He says he does not know where Hoyt is," said Du Pré.

"And he could be telling the truth," said Pidgeon. "He could even be truthful about all of it. It doesn't make me happy to say so, but he could be."

"Maybe he saves Hoyt's life," said Du Pré.

"Maybe," said Pidgeon, "but if Vardaman gets through this OK, then *he* has Temple Security to worry about. The big snake's head is cut off, but we don't know how many others there are."

A dark sedan came down the street, fast, and turned into the parking lot. It nosed into a space and four men got out. One of them waved at Pidgeon and Du Pré. He walked over while the others went inside the county building.

"Fun, fun, fun," said Harvey.

"Yeah," said Pidgeon.

Du Pré nodded at him.

"Whaddaya think, Pidge?" said Harvey.

"I think Vardaman is a very smart guy, is what I think," said Pidgeon. "I also think we're wasting our time. Hoyt has no reason to be here now—if he ever was here. Why don't you go fishing?"

Harvey looked at Du Pré, who nodded.

"We got nothing else?" said Harvey.

"Not a thing," said Pidgeon.

"You go through the vehicles Cutler and company were driving?" said Harvey.

Pidgeon looked at him. "I'm but a consultant," she said. "Go talk to the special agent in charge."

"OK," said Harvey.

"He's the idiot in the bright blue shirt with the white collar and cuffs and the red suspenders so we know he went to Harvard," said Pidgeon. "I don't know if he really did, but he sure would like me to think so."

"All right, all right," said Harvey.

"You asked me to come," said Pidgeon.

"Crime just isn't the same without you, Pidge," said Harvey.

"Call me Pidge once more and I'll ram your nuts up your windpipe," said Pidgeon. "Now fuck off and go in there with the rubber hose and get us something we can use to bring down the rest of Temple Security . . ."

Harvey smiled at her, fondly.

"That's my girl," he said, walking toward the front door.

"They can't hold all of them forever," said Pidgeon.

Du Pré nodded.

A cold breeze was sloughing down from the mountains. Pidgeon shivered.

"Whatever happens here," she said, "this isn't over. Vardaman is squarely in their sights now. Killing Cutler won't put an end to Temple. They're strong in the Lord, there, and they are blood mean . . ."

"Vardaman knows that," said Du Pré.

Pidgeon looked at him.

"He said he would help us save Hoyt," said Du Pré. "And for now, he has done that."

Pidgeon nodded.

"Maybe I'll look at Vardaman's computer again," she said. "We can impound it for a while."

"He knows where Hoyt is," said Du Pré. "Vardaman does."

Du Pré rolled a smoke and lit it and Pidgeon walked back into the county building.

· Chapter 37 ·

THE SPECIAL AGENT in charge looked with distaste at a spot on his white cuff. He touched it, frowning.

"All yours," he said. "I wish my daughter hadn't given me this fucking shirt. It was a birthday present. It's beautifully made. She got it in London, when she was there with her mother. It will last forever. I hate this fucking shirt. She gave me the red suspenders, too."

Pidgeon guffawed.

"So anyway," he said, "I am more than happy to give you Banner Vardaman. He wants us to believe that he is but a simple redneck, capable of little more than doing sums and fixing flat tires. The son of a bitch was having the best old time with us in there."

"Hard one," said Harvey.

"Well," said the agent, "we only catch the dumb ones, you know. If they're smart, as many are, they get away scot-free. They reach high office. They become rich."

"Agent Bradley," said Harvey, "you did your best."

"Oh, don't I know it," said the agent. "Now home to lovely Butte to run down leads on Jimmy Hoffa's grave site and other important tasks. I'm more than happy to hand all this over to you, Agent Wallace. I'm a humble man of humble aspirations and this mess is something I'm afraid will grow larger before becoming completely preposterous. It's that sort of time here in America . . ."

"I was rude to you," said Pidgeon. "I apologize."

"Oh," said Agent Bradley, "no need. Agent Samantha Pidgeon is a legend in the Federal Bureau of Investigation. To have been insulted by you is an honor. Truth to tell, if I saw me, I'd think I was what you thought I was . . ."

Pidgeon laughed.

"What's even worse," said Agent Bradley, "is that I am in fact what you thought that I was, which I try to forget. But my daughter is a snob as only a fourteen-year-old in braces and clothes like those worn by Boston's Combat Zone hookers can be. I seemed to be sliding inexorably into either the family brokerage or the law firm and I thought I would try to do something for my country. Perhaps pursue the worst of the white-collar criminals, since so many of them are relations of mine. But no, I'm here, making cases against crank cookers and drug importers. I think that stuff should be legal and taxed. I don't fit in anywhere. But enough about me. If you need anything I can help with, do call. I'm not as worried about getting fired as many of us are. You want job security, let 'em know you don't care if they do fire you . . ."

"I will call," said Pidgeon.

"Good," said Bradley. "And if you find a way to fuck up that lot of fascists in Temple Security, and I can help, be sure to call."

He shrugged into his sport coat and he went out, whistling.

"Well," said Harvey, "that was refreshing."

Du Pré yawned. He looked at his watch. La Salle was in the interrogation room with Vardaman.

Two FBI agents came sprinting past Harvey, Pidgeon, and Du Pré, and both of them had machine pistols, and they ran to the end of the hall, opened the door, and screamed, "ON THE FLOOR!"

"That's interesting," said Pidgeon.

They watched one agent hold his machine pistol on the people on the floor while the other agent frisked them very thoroughly.

Harvey wandered down the hall.

"Need any help?" he said.

"I think we've got this," said the agent who was not doing the frisking, "but God knows what else there is to find. Go on out to the lot. Find the three black Suburbans this bunch came in. One of the techs there will fill you in."

Harvey nodded, turned, walked back to Pidgeon and Du Pré. They went out the side door and down the steps.

The three Suburbans were at the far end of the paved lot. All had their hoods up and there were piles of assorted objects on the pavement next to them.

Five people in blue FBI windbreakers were taking the interiors of the vehicles apart.

"Whatcha got?" said Harvey, holding out his ID to the nearest agent.

The agent looked at the card and then at Harvey. "Various toys," he said. "The really interesting one is over there . . ." and he pointed at a silver can. It was about the size of a gallon paint can and had a wire bail. Two small glass jars sat next to it, each in a plastic bag, with a timer and some odd pieces of wire and molded material in a heap to the side.

"Jesus," said Pidgeon.

"Is that what I think it is?" said Harvey over his shoulder.

"Yep," said the agent, looking up from a door panel he was removing. "There are three others, as well. We've disarmed the stuff, but I wouldn't fuck with any of it unless you know what you're doing."

"OK," said Du Pré, "what am I looking at?"

"Cyanide generators," said Harvey.

"You could kill everyone in a large supermarket with one of these," said Pidgeon. "Or an airport baggage claim, or a high school basketball game."

"What they have these for?" said Du Pré.

"Those are questions," said Harvey, "we would like to know the answers to, very much . . ."

"Ted found the can," said the agent from over the door panel, "and he decided to open it. He set it down *very* carefully and then we started taking everything apart looking for the other pieces of the generator."

"I would think so," said Pidgeon.

"It was well designed," said the agent.

"Anything else?" said Harvey.

The agent looked up again. "In our van," he said. "Show your ID to Cassie and ask her for the mileage boosters."

Pidgeon sucked in her breath.

She and Harvey went to the FBI van, a big one with wire-mesh window glass and huge wide tires.

Du Pré followed.

A young woman got down from the back of the van.

"It's OK, Cassie," the agent called.

The young woman spoke with Harvey for a moment.

She went into the van and she came out with something in her fist. She opened her hand and Pidgeon picked up a small gray metal object. It was a half cylinder about the size of a plum.

Du Pré looked at it. "What is it?" he said.

"It's a small shaped charge," said Pidgeon. "Iranian. Activated by a cell phone." She pointed to a little black square. "You program it there," she said.

Du Pré nodded.

"This is what set off the explosion that almost got you," she said.

"No timer," said Du Pré.

"You can use this for a timer," said Pidgeon. "Works either way."

"I see why our friends inside were so wound up," said Harvey.

"Oh, yeah," said Pidgeon.

"Hah," said the agent who had been stripping the panels from the door of the Suburban. He carefully lifted out a grayish tube about two inches in diameter and a foot long. "Plastique," said the agent.

La Salle and Vardaman came down the side steps.

They walked over to where Harvey and Pidgeon and Du Pré stood.

Vardaman glanced at the stuff on the ground.

"Give the people an enemy they fear," he said, "and you can then do what you want with them."

La Salle and Du Pré looked at him.

"Hermann Goering," said Vardaman. "And you know, it worked . . . very well."

He looked up at the summer sky, blue and puffed with clouds. "Beautiful day," he said, "but I think it's gonna rain . . ."

· **Chapter 38** ·

SNOW SNAKES WOUND across the highway, hissing.

Du Pré looked at the western sky, the color of metal, steel, cold.

"My, my," said Jack La Salle, "what a nice January day not to fly."

"The Denver Airport is closed again," said Pidgeon. "It shuts down a lot. I've never understood Denver. Why is it there? At all?"

"Good question," said La Salle. "But here in the good old U S of A the answer always comes back to a whole lot of money . . ."

Fine flakes of snow began to fall, thick, dancing in the wind. Pidgeon gunned the engine, slewed around a semi that was only going eighty-five.

She pulled back in. They rode in silence for a while.

Then the signs for Denver's exits began to appear, and Pidgeon put the Suburban down a ramp, swerving from side to side on the new snow. She barely stopped at the bottom. "Fuckin' snow," she said.

"I'm walking home," said La Salle.

"Wussy," said Pidgeon.

La Salle turned and he looked at Du Pré. "You really think Hoyt might be here in Denver?" he said.

Du Pré shrugged.

"The guy is very good," said La Salle. "We have had some awfully thorough people looking for him for months and there's no trace . . ."

. . . Hoyt Poe up in smoke . . . or dead maybe . . . these are ver' bad people . . .

As Pidgeon squinted at the street signs, she roared around a car that was going too slow for her liking, then whipped back into the lane. Oncoming traffic honked horns. Pidgeon gave them the finger.

She turned off into a parking garage. Grabbing a time ticket, she stuck it in the ashtray, which was full of butts.

La Salle fished it out and clipped it to the sun visor.

Pidgeon parked.

"Driving with you, m'dear," said La Salle, "is worse than combat."

They got out, pulling on warm coats.

"Du Pré," said Pidgeon, "security is very tight here. You haven't got a knife in your boot or anything, do you?"

Du Pré grinned, pulled the knife out of his right boot. He put it in the Suburban.

"He did that just to mess with you," said La Salle.

Pidgeon walked up to the car's hood, paused, and then they went down to ground level in an elevator that stank of piss.

There was a screen site set up in the lobby of the Federal Building. They went through one by one.

There was another at the entrance to the courtroom.

A woman with short blond hair and five men were sitting at a long table, with four attorneys.

The prosecutor's table was empty.

La Salle looked at the clock on the right wall. He looked at Pidgeon.

She shook her head slowly.

The clock read five minutes to one.

At three minutes to one two men came in, in three-piece suits, and each carried a slender briefcase. They stood at the prosecutor's table. The bailiff called the court to order.

The judge entered, looked at the two men at the prosecutor's table. The judge was heavy, white-haired, ruddy-faced.

One of the prosecutors cleared his throat. "If Your Honor please," he said, "I replaced US Attorney Karcher at nine this morning and I have not had time to review the documents pertaining to this case . . ."

The judge looked at him. "So," said the judge, "you're asking for a postponement of the trial, obviously."

"I have to have time to prepare," said the prosecutor.

"You have a name, sir?" said the judge.

"US Attorney Willetts," said the prosecutor.

The judge steepled his fingers. He looked off into the distance.

"Those bastards," hissed Pidgeon.

"Bailiff?" said the judge.

The bailiff strode forward, stood in front of the bench.

"If US Attorney Karcher and, I assume, all his assistants were replaced an hour ago," said the judge, "I would suppose they are busy cleaning out their desks, wouldn't you?"

"They are," said the bailiff.

"Go get 'em," said the judge, "and have Rodney and Louis arrest these two impostors at the prosecutor's table."

"Your Honor!" yelled the lead prosecutor. "This is . . ."

Two huge men in blue uniforms came in, one white, one black.

"Those two," said the judge. "Make sure you mumble their rights at them."

The two men at the prosecutor's table stood, mouths open, and then they were dragged through a side door.

"Your Honor!" yelled one of the defense attorneys.

"Shut up, Bob," said the judge, "or I'll throw you into the basement for Igor to play with. I never saw such crap in all my life . . ."

The blond woman turned round, her face white with fury.

Seven people, four men and three women, all in suits and all looking stricken, filed through the door. They walked to the prosecutor's table.

"Mister Karcher," said the judge, "I was just now informed that you were fired, sir. And did that happen this morning?"

"Yes," said a broad, short man with a head of gray curls.

"And how was this firing brought about?" said the judge.

"I received a telephone call from Washington, Your Honor," said Karcher.

"Fired your assistants too?" said the judge.

"Yes, Your Honor," said Karcher.

The judge nodded.

"Couple fellows came in here," said the judge, "and told me quite a fairy tale, and so, since they were obviously impostors and party to a practical joke not in keeping with the gravity of this court, I arrested them for contempt . . ."

Karcher stared at the judge.

"So you didn't get a formal letter?" said the judge.

"No, Your Honor," said Karcher.

"Just a phone call," said the judge.

"Yes, Your Honor," said Karcher.

The other six people at the prosecutor's table were now grinning at one another.

"Hoo-boy," said Pidgeon.

"Well," said the judge, "why don't we see if we can get your six months' worth of files up here . . ."

The doors opened and a white-haired woman in a blue suit pushed a cart into the courtroom. It was piled high with folders.

"And that looks just like what we need," said the judge. "Now, Bob, I want you to come up here and put your hand on that Bible and swear to tell the truth . . ."

The lead defense attorney approached the bench, put his hand on the Bible offered by the bailiff, and took the oath.

"Now, Bob," said the judge, "you and I know that this trial venue has been changed once, spurious motions by the truckload have been filed, and now I want you to tell me if you knew about these firings before nine o'clock this morning . . ."

The attorney looked like something was stuck in his throat.

"Bearing in mind that there are serious sanctions for perjury," said the judge, "and not to mention that it would really piss me off."

The attorney swallowed.

"I take it that means yes?" said the judge.

The attorney nodded.

"Now," said the judge, "you will be forthright and tell me just when you learned of this business of replacing Karcher and his people with the folks I just had arrested?"

"Five weeks ago," said the attorney.

"Five weeks," said the judge. "You know, that suggests to me a conspiracy to pervert justice. Loudly. Very loudly."

The judge looked at the defendants and their attorneys and back to the prosecutor. "Proceed, Mister Karcher," said the judge. "And you see that flag over there? We are now going to do something that honors that flag, sir."

· Chapter 39 ·

THEY WALKED UP to the green Suburban, and Pidgeon looked at La Salle.

"Right," he said. He lay down on the concrete and he slid under the big vehicle.

Du Pré did the same, at the back. They both took small flashlights from their pockets and played the beam across the undercarriage.

Pidgeon looked at the hood, carefully. "The hair's still here," she said, pulling it off.

"Seems OK underneath," said La Salle. He and Du Pré crawled back out.

"After what I just saw in there," said Pidgeon, "I'll be checking out my transportation from now on."

"What you just saw in there," said La Salle, "was a man brave enough to say enough is enough."

A small sedan with dark windows parked across the traffic lane blinked its lights once.

Du Pré looked at it. The license plates were from New Mexico.

The driver's door opened and a man got out. He had a beard and dark glasses and he wore a turtleneck sweater and ski pants and zippered nylon boots.

The man looked left and then he looked right. "How you all doin'?" said Bobby Don Poe.

Du Pré looked at him.

"It's me, Bobby Don," said Bobby Don, "disguised as some yuppie from Taos. There are damn few ski hills where I was fetched up . . ." He walked over to them.

"I followed you in here," he said, "and no one came near your rig. Good idea to check, though . . ."

"Christ," said La Salle, "we've been trying to get hold of you."

"Us Poes," said Bobby Don, "well, we do a couple things mostly, the men anyhow. The military and jail. Lot of us do both, come to think on it. So we're artful at not tellin' anyone ain't a Poe anything about any Poe . . ."

"I thought you might be dead," said La Salle.

"I'm kinda surprised I'm not," said Bobby Don. "Each day is a new wonder. Now what the hell went on in there? I just heard a blip on the radio sayin' TV vans were stacked up in front of the Federal Building . . ."

"A judge decided to cause problems for our government," said La Salle. "We might even get our country back if we're lucky."

"Did he now?" said Bobby Don.

"Someone in the administration decided to fire the US attorney trying this case on the opening day of the trial," said La Salle. "The judge wasn't having it."

Bobby Don nodded. "I'll try to stay hopeful," he said. "How's Banner?"

"Making fly rods," said La Salle, "but his place is now a fortress."

"Banner's a tough one," said Bobby Don. "So he got off on the shootin's?"

"There was no evidence," said La Salle, "that suggested anything other than what he said happened: self-defense. And, of course, it helps that the locals there are fond of him and not fond of outsiders."

"Temple's got a lot of problems at the moment," said Bobby Don. "I would imagine they're clearing computers and burning papers at a right good clip."

"And no word from Hoyt?" said La Salle.

"I did get some word from Hoyt and I wanted to tell you about it," said Bobby Don. "Now I suggest we climb into your rig. I don't like just standin' around in public with famous folks . . ."

They all got into the Suburban.

Bobby Don took a folded sheet of paper from his pocket and he looked at it for a long time.

"Hoyt isn't the brightest feller I ever knew," said Bobby Don, "but he could do in a pinch. He sent a package to our Aunt Bea with a note, askin' her to keep the package secret. Said it was a Christmas present for me. Aunt Bea is a woman cut in from the same cloth as our Grannie Dulcie, so that is just exactly what she done. I thought, of course, if I loped on home for the holidays that it might not be too healthy, so it took till the first week of January here to get the package to me. It had a lot of money in it, which is very handy for a feller in my position. Had this note too."

La Salle and Du Pré and Pidgeon looked at Bobby Don, who unfolded the sheet of paper.

"'Dear Cuz,'" read Bobby Don, "'I expect you knew what I was up to, and after you let me off in Denver I found a cheap room in a place that don't ask questions and I got a bottle and drank it while I thought about what it was I was going to do. When the car blew up with Sandy and little Faith Helen in it, it went so fast they didn't have time to scream. But I dream about it and I see them, and they're screaming but with no sound, just their mouths open and flames all around them. I wanted to kill a bunch of folks, starting with that son of a bitch Lloyd Cutler, and after I was sober again I decided I had best go and pray about it, like Granny Dulcie used to tell us, you remember? So I went out and found this big stone church, it was open, and I went in and there was no one else there. It had real pretty stained-glass windows and a lot of fancy stuff up front, not like what we have to home. And I sat there, praying a little, and thought, well, I done what they asked me to do and I got shot up, and I testified as to crimes I had seen. And then I thought about what I might've seen in that restaurant parking lot and I all of a sudden knew I seen that woman once before, at the prison outside of Kabul, just once, but when you are hurt bad you remember better, I guess. So I sat there and this old man come in the church on a crutch, had but one leg, and he sat up front and he prayed and I suddenly knowed what I wanted to do. I figured I would die if I tried to kill those people, but that was what I wanted even more than I wanted them dead, and God would find them anyway, in his own time. So after a while I went back to the room and got my stuff and took a cab out to where I could thumb it. Two rides and I made it to Billings, where I am mailing this to you. I will make my way back to them mountains behind Mr. and Mrs. Fascelli's ranch. Tell Mister Du Pré I am at the little old church, one that is falling down, he will know the one, and I will put oil on his rifle and wrap it good in plastic so it don't rust. I got to do this, while I am strong, because I still want to kill them people and if I do that then I am as bad as they are. You should have this note after Christmas, I trust Aunt Bea to do what I asked. I ain't that strong, so I think I had best go and be with Sandy and Faith Helen and my daddy and Granny Dulcie. Hoyt.'"

"Jesus Christ," said Pidgeon.

"Yeah," said Bobby Don. "Everybody kind of sold Hoyt out. I guess he didn't want no more."

Pidgeon looked at Du Pré.

"You know where he meant?" she said.

Du Pré nodded. "Yes," he said, "I know where."

Jack La Salle was staring off into the far distance.

"You could come back with us," said Pidgeon, looking at Bobby Don.

He shook his head.

"I wouldn't want to be a bother, ma'am," said Bobby Don.

"You come," said Du Pré. "You come and we will go and find Hoyt and we will bury him. And you go over, work with Banner."

"I can't stand Banner," said Bobby Don.

"Right. And he hates you too," said Pidgeon. "Cut it out."

"Well," said Bobby Don, "you put it that way."

"I do," said Pidgeon. "Taos. Christ."

"It is a strange place," said Bobby Don. "Lot of rich people complainin' all the time 'bout how unhappy they are . . ."

"Get your stuff," said Pidgeon.

Bobby Don walked to the sedan, opened the trunk, took out a big traveling case, the sort that has a handle and wheels. He got an old leather briefcase from the front and put all of it in the back of the Suburban.

He got in. Du Pré handed him a whiskey bottle.

"Don't mind I do," said Bobby Don.

"The car yours?" said La Salle.

"That thing?" said Bobby Don. "It belongs to some rich asshole needed something to be unhappy about."

"Is it clean?" said La Salle.

"Oh, yes," said Bobby Don, "I am downright meticulous."

Pidgeon drove down the ramp and out on to the street. She turned and gathered speed and she headed north on the interstate.

The snowsnakes writhed and hissed.

"Another storm comin'," said Bobby Don.

"No," said La Salle. "It's already here."

· Chapter 40 ·

THE SNOW ON the field was a foot or so deep, and the Suburbans wallowed as they crossed it, moving toward the slumped little church that had once been white, before the painters died or moved away. The roof had fallen in on the north side, and the door in the little vestibule hung only by the bottom hinge.

Du Pré came up close as he could to it and he stopped the big SUV and the other stopped behind him.

Benny Klein looked at Du Pré.

"Well," said Benny, "I'm the coroner too." He looked like he was going to puke.

"I will go in," said Du Pré. "If he is dead, he is dead, I will tell you that he is dead."

"We got to identify him," said Benny.

"The state lab will do that," said Du Pré, "if I cannot." He took a heavy black plastic body bag from the backseat.

"I come too," said Madelaine. Her rosary was in her hands.

La Salle and Bobby Don Poe and Father Van Den Heuvel and Pidgeon got out of the other Suburban.

Du Pré saw movement at the corner of his eye. A big yellow-gray coyote was running flat out. Its tracks led back to the little broken church.

"Who were the people who built this?" said La Salle.

"Norwegians," said Du Pré, "came here, homesteaded, tried to make it raising wheat. They did not last very long . . ." La Salle nodded.

Pallas got out of the back of Du Pré's SUV. She carried a long twist of sweetgrass.

A crumpled rusted Land Rover came up the tracks the Suburbans had just made. It halted.

Banner Vardaman got out, and four other men, all wearing army uniforms.

POE, POE, POE, DENTON, said the name tags above their shirt pockets.

"What's the drill here?" said Vardaman.

"I go in," said Du Pré, "I am a deputy, make a statement later, if there is any question about who he is, remains have to go to the state lab."

"It's cold," said Vardaman. "We'll wait in the Rover."

"The goddamned heater don't work, Ban," said one of the Poes.

"Always complainin', them Poes," said Vardaman.

"Get in one of the Suburbans," said La Salle. "We'll signal you if it's time . . ."

The men scrambled into the warm SUV. Including Vardaman.

Du Pré went to the door, pushed, it was stuck in snow and ice. He pulled and the hinge popped out and he worked the door back and forth until it came free.

There was a tall package wrapped in black plastic beside the door.

Du Pré lifted it, handed it to La Salle, who carried it to the SUV and put it in the back.

There was a second door, farther in, but when Du Pré pulled it, it swung open with no difficulty. The roof had collapsed but the doorposts were still true.

It was both light and dark inside, the sun bright on some of the big room, and pieces of the roof above casting shadows deep and black on others.

There was a mounded pile of snow beneath the biggest of the roof holes.

Du Pré turned on his flashlight, pointed the beam at the snowy heap, saw the skull.

The jawbone was gone.

He walked over, shone the light more closely.

A few rags, an army uniform once, around a lump.

Du Pré saw a black chain of small beads, tugged it.

Dog tags.

Poe, Hoyt and the numbers and the O-positive blood type.

A cross, small and stamped in the metal.

A wallet in what would have been a pocket of the pants.

Hoyt Poe's driver's license.

A faded photograph of Sandy holding little Faith Helen, a baby.

Du Pré continued to look, found a boot with a bone sticking up from it, all the flesh gone and the marks of coyote and skunk teeth in it.

He went back out.

He nodded.

Vardaman and the men got out and came to him.

"He was mostly eaten by coyotes, skunks, badgers," said Du Pré, "so he is just bones. There is a skull. No jawbone, hole in the right temple . . ."

"God. Damn. Them," said Vardaman.

"If it is all the same to you," said one of the Poes, "we'll get the bones."

Vardaman and Bobby Don went with them.

Father Van Den Heuvel and Madelaine were standing

together, praying silently. Their lips moved, as did their fingers on their rosary beads.

Du Pré opened the door of the SUV.

"It is him," said Du Pré. "Bullet hole in the skull, Hoyt Poe's dog tags and driver's license . . ."

Benny scribbled on a form held on a clipboard.

"I suppose," he said, "they got any questions, they can ask them."

"Poe," said Du Pré, "he was here all along, mostly."

Jack La Salle had wandered off a hundred feet or so. He was looking up at the mountains; there were tears trickling down his cheeks. Du Pré walked over to him. "You remember the inscription on the monument at Thermopylae?" said La Salle.

"Yes," said Du Pré.

"Traveler, if you should come to Sparta, tell them that we lie here in obedience to their laws."

"We couldn't save him," said La Salle. "He was a good man, he did what he thought was the right thing, and those fuckers who wanted to have their war just because they could, sold him out. They sold all of us out . . ."

"Yah," said Du Pré.

"He does the right thing about our laws being broken and he sees his wife and child incinerated. He wants revenge but knows that that is wrong, too, so he kills himself. It was all that he has left," said La Salle, "and the worst thing about all this is knowing that it can and will happen again. And again . . ."

"Yah," said Du Pré.

"You found his bones?" said La Salle.

"There are some there," said Du Pré. "Others are carried away, never will be found."

They walked back to Madelaine and Father Van Den Heuvel and Pallas. Pallas had lit the sweetgrass twist, the lovely smoke curled toward heaven.

"It's cold," said Madelaine.

They went to the Suburban, got in, Du Pré started the engine and the heater pumped away.

Vardaman came out of the ruined church; he waved and walked over.

Du Pré rolled down his window.

Vardaman handed Du Pré his missing Glock. Du Pré looked at it, pulled back the slide; the chamber was empty.

"Here's the clip," said Vardaman, handing it to Du Pré. "It was on a window ledge. Hoyt just had the one in the chamber . . ."

Du Pré looked at him.

"We hold bein' safe with guns in high esteem," said Vardaman. "Knowin' Hoyt, he woulda done it that way, case some kid found the gun . . ."

"God," said Madelaine, and she began to cry.

"I am so sorry," said Jack La Salle.

"We know that, General," said Vardaman. "It sure ain't the likes of you caused this . . ."

Benny shifted in his seat. "You want to take the remains," he said, "go ahead. I done my report."

"Obliged," said Vardaman. "I guess his kin will take them back and put them down next to Sandy and Faith Helen and Dulcie. Hoyt and Dulcie did always get on."

"I would like to have known her," said La Salle.

"She was a good one," said Vardaman. "Dulcie was one of them people had a light around her, fer sure . . ."

The men in the old uniforms came out. One of them carried the body bag, with not a lot in it.

They all left then.

Du Pré drove back to the main ranch, and no one said anything at all.

Chapter 41

PALLAS RODE STEWBALL around the Toussaint Saloon, whooping. She was wearing clothes that Idries had brought from Kazakhstan. She was swathed in impossibly lovely silk brocades and furs of sable, fox, and marten. She had high pale brown boots, and a wide belt.

She looked bright as the spring sun and she looked happy. She was soon to fly halfway around the world and live as people had lived there for millennia with their horses, hounds, hawks, and hunters, under the great sky. Many people had come down from Canada or from the east, the Dakotas.

Pallas was going a long way for a long time and she might never return. Idries was riding Walkin' John, who had a good horselaugh as he passed by Du Pré.

Du Pré was standing at the back of the saloon's old porch, looking up at the Wolf Mountains and smoking.

Lourdes was having a hard time with her twin sister's leaving. They weren't identical but they were very close, although Pallas was bold and outgoing and Lourdes was quiet and orderly.

Lourdes was riding Moondog, one of the two racing horses bought long ago so Du Pré could slide into the shadowy world of brush racing, illegal betting arrangements out in the weeds, where horse fanciers put up big money on their stock, and sometimes killed each other over gambling debts or alcohol-fueled arguments.

She was trying loyally to act happy for her happy sister, but she was so open-faced, hiding her true emotions was impossible for her.

She rode up to Du Pré and she swung down. Moondog had a lot of fizz, so he danced a little where he stood. Lourdes finally put him in the pole corral the bar had kept from the days when people rode in for a drink. It still got a lot of use. Moondog had a nice cold drink of water and then he watched Lourdes.

"I want to be happy for her, Granpère," she said, "but I don't feel happy. She is my sister and she is a lot better at everything than I am, I have been jealous about that all my life, and now she is going away and I know that I will be only half of myself."

"Pallas is not better than you are at everything," said Du Pré, "she is just noisier about what she is good at. You are a very good hand with horses. You love them and they know it. And you are a great cook; Pallas does not cook so Idries has a surprise coming to him."

They both laughed.

"I am a better fiddler," said Lourdes.

"Yah," said Du Pré, "much better, lots better."

They laughed. Pallas had never even tried to play anything.

"She was always the crazy one," said Lourdes, "she got a lot of attention. She liked that I think."

"And now she is going where she truly belongs," said Du Pre.

Pallas rode past on Stewball. She swung down and pulled the headstall from Stewball and put him in the pole corral, still saddled. Stewball and Moondog were good friends.

Pallas walked up to them.

"Lourdes," she said, "I will miss you and you must come and visit. We can ride on the great grassland country of Kazakhstan. You can come and hunt with eagles."

Lourdes smiled. "I will come," she said, "I will . . ." and the twin sisters hugged each other, tears streaming down their faces. They cried a long time.

"It is so far," said Lourdes, "but our people walked all that way so long ago. Long time gone . . ."

Idries rode to the corral on Walkin' John and he put him in and came to Du Pré and the twins.

Pallas hugged him and then they stood, arms around each other, happy.

"Does Mukhtar Khan have an eagle for me yet?" said Pallas.

"It is not that simple," said Idries, "you have to be ready for the eagle. To hunt an eagle takes a great skill. Mukhtar can talk to them, so they don't break his arm with their talons. They are very strong birds and first he will have you flying smaller birds, maybe a falcon."

"OK," said Pallas.

"Idries," said Du Pré, "when Pallas says that it is OK she means she has seen the way around you and will do just what she wants."

They all laughed.

They went in the back door of the saloon, which was packed with people all talking as loud as they could so no one could hear anyone and take offense.

Du Pré made his way to the bandstand and he found Bassman and Père Godin already there and tuned, so Du Pré pulled his fiddle from the case and he drew the bow over the strings and they did a slow version of "The Buffalo Star" and people began to dance and the racket faded.

A lot of food had been brought in and Susan Klein also had a table with roast beef and ham and fried chicken on it, and the guests were making away with it fairly rapidly.

Du Pré saw Lourdes out of the corner of his eye, she had her fiddle and she was nodding her head in time to the music. He motioned to her, but she shook her head.

Bassman walked over to her, still playing his bass, which had some impossible dingus in it that meant he needed no cord. He said something to Lourdes and she looked startled and then she came up on the stage with Du Pré and Père Godin.

Lourdes began "Baptiste's Lament" and Du Pré played along for a few bars, then stood back and watched his granddaughter fiddle.

They played for an hour or so, and when they stopped and went outside to cool off they saw Raymond and Jacqueline and Pallas and Idries together.

"We must go," said Idries. "We are flying out of Seattle and we have to go through a lot before we take off."

The moment was here, and everyone got quiet and then Idries and Pallas walked to the SUV and they got in and the big vehicle pulled away.

. . . maybe I don't see her again . . . maybe . . .

And then Du Pré and Lourdes went back inside to make music.

· Chapter 42 ·

MADELAINE CAME OUT of the kitchen with four platters, two on each arm, and she made her way to a table and set them down and she went back and got more.

The Toussaint Saloon was filled with the Friday crowd, all hungry for good aged beef.

"Who're we eatin' tonight?" said a rancher as she passed.

"Percy and Cuthbert," said Madelaine, over her shoulder.

Du Pré sat at the big table with Banner Vardaman and Bobby Don Poe, Pidgeon, Bart, and Benetsee. Benetsee had suffered Madelaine's total war on his person and clothing and was wearing clean new jeans, high boots made of nylon that closed with Velcro clasps, and a new flannel shirt.

His white braids were newly done and wrapped with red cloth. Susan Klein and Madelaine brought huge platters of prime ribs of beef and double-baked potatoes and a giant bowl of salad.

Du Pré had a bottle of whiskey by his place and a carafe of ice water and there were several bottles of red wine, and a half-gallon of screw-top pink for Benetsee.

"I thank you again," said Bobby Don, looking at Bart and Pidgeon.

"When it calms down," said Bart, "and it will, you can come back."

"I might," said Bobby Don, "and then I might just stay over there. I like what I hear of those Kazakhs. I like the camels. I like the eagles and the horses, and I like that country. Damned big country."

"Idries will look out for you," said Bart. "He's a good man."

Benetsee drank a large glass of his awful jug wine. He belched. He attacked the slab of rare beef.

"Eat the spud, the salad," said Madelaine, passing by. "You don't live on booze and raw meat."

"We live on raw meat for a long time," said Benetsee, irritated. But Madelaine was long gone.

Bobby Don pulled a sheaf of papers from his coat and he handed them to Du Pré.

Photographs.

Hoyt Poe's coffin, the soldiers who were his honor guard. Pictures taken at the wake. Robust people, laughing. Hoyt Poe's grave.

"Thought you might like these," said Bobby Don. "It's as much of an end as we get . . ."

Du Pré nodded.

"I try and train this young'un," said Banner Vardaman, "give him a trade to practice in life, and then he just goes and runs off . . ."

"Oh, fer Chrissakes," said Bobby Don, "I got better things to do with m' life than make fish poles for rich fucks . . ."

"It's a good solid trade," said Banner.

"Fish poles for rich fucks," said Bobby Don. "I'm going to ride with the people who grabbed them the biggest empire the world has ever known."

"Tha's nothin'," said Banner, "next to a good fly rod."

"You don't want nobody in your goddamned shop anyway," said Bobby Don, "except you, you cranky son of a bitch."

"I hadn't thought of it that way," said Vardaman. "But you're right."

"There were more indictments today," said Bart. "Be more next week, too."

"It's a start," said Pidgeon, grimly.

"Does your lawyer, that Mr. Foote," said Bobby Don, "really have to go to Kazakhstan?"

"He does," said Bart. "He does indeed. Beats having to send things regular mail. So it's no trouble to take you along. He'll meet you at the Billlings airport."

"Well, I appreciate it," said Bobby Don. "I don't like those Russian planes. They're rickety."

"When you get there," said Bart, "stick to horses and camels."

They finished eating and Madelaine brought out a big chocolate cake, one that showed ruby red at the seams.

"Whoo boy," said Bart, "chocolate and raspberries."

The windows rattled.

Another blizzard had come in, cold and fierce.

Du Pré went back to the photographs.

One was in black and white, unlike all the others, of a woman in a high-necked lace blouse and a dark suit, holding a hymnal. She had light hair and pale eyes.

"That's Dulcie," said Bobby Don, "when she was young, about maybe 1930. She's wearing her grandma's blouse and dress. It was green velvet."

Du Pré looked at the picture for a long time.

Dulcie had been beautiful, and there was a lift to one corner of her mouth, which made her even lovelier, less severe. She had high cheekbones and a large mouth, and hands with very long graceful fingers.

"She was a good woman," said Du Pré.

Bobby Don nodded. "Like I said, she had this light about her. She . . . found the good in people and made them live up to it. I never knew no one like her, but her . . ."

Du Pré nodded.

"She did good things for you," said Du Pré.

"Yes," said Bobby Don, "she did. She died eight years ago when she was eighty-six, and so many people come, people we never suspected even knew her. They all come, they was all happy and sad at once, you know, happy that they had been lucky enough to know her and sad 'cause she was gone."

They all ate slices of cake except Benetsee.

The old man had more wine and another piece of rare beef.

"Are you really planning to drive back to Billings in this crap?" said Bart, looking at Vardaman and then at the windows, which were shuddering in their frames.

"The Land Rover," said Banner Vardaman, "is immortal. It has just three hundred thousand miles on it. It goes forward. It backs up. This is all that I ask of a vehicle."

"I'd feel better if you took one of the new Suburbans," said Bart.

"And hurt Em'ly's feelin's?" said Vardaman.

Bart threw up his hands.

They finished their meal and went out into the snow.

Du Pré looked to the west. There was a band of half-light there, so the storm was breaking up.

Bobby Don and Vardaman got into the Rover.

Banner turned the key, the engine hummed.

He flicked on lights.

A fan roared.

Benetsee came out of the saloon, wearing an odd hat with a high point on the top and long furred earflaps. He had on a bulky leather coat.

"Well," said Vardaman. "See y'all."

He backed and turned and was gone in the swirling snow in seconds.

Du Pré turned round.

Benetsee was gone.

Bart and Pidgeon looked at Du Pré.

"He was right here," said Bart, "and then he wasn't . . ."

Du Pré shrugged.

They went back inside.

A moon rose later, half full, glowing on the horizon.

Driving home Du Pré saw a great gray owl float silently over the driven snow, and then it was gone in shadow.

· ABOUT THE AUTHOR ·

Peter Bowen (b. 1945) is an author best known for mystery novels set in the modern American West. When he was ten, Bowen's family moved to Bozeman, Montana, where a paper route introduced him to the grizzled old cowboys who frequented a bar called The Oaks. Listening to their stories, some of which stretched back to the 1870s, Bowen found inspiration for his later fiction.

Following time at the University of Michigan and the University of Montana, Bowen published his first novel, *Yellowstone Kelly*, in 1987. After two more novels featuring the real-life Western hero, Bowen published *Coyote Wind* (1994), which introduced Gabriel Du Pré, a mixed-race lawman living in fictional Toussaint, Montana. Bowen has written thirteen novels in the series, in which Du Pré gets tangled up in everything from cold-blooded murder to the hunt for rare fossils. Bowen continues to live and write in Livingston, Montana.

THE MONTANA MYSTERIES
FEATURING GABRIEL DU PRÉ

FROM OPEN ROAD MEDIA

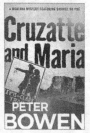

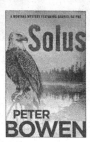

INTEGRATED MEDIA

Find a full list of our authors and
titles at www.openroadmedia.com

FOLLOW US
@OpenRoadMedia